AF258479

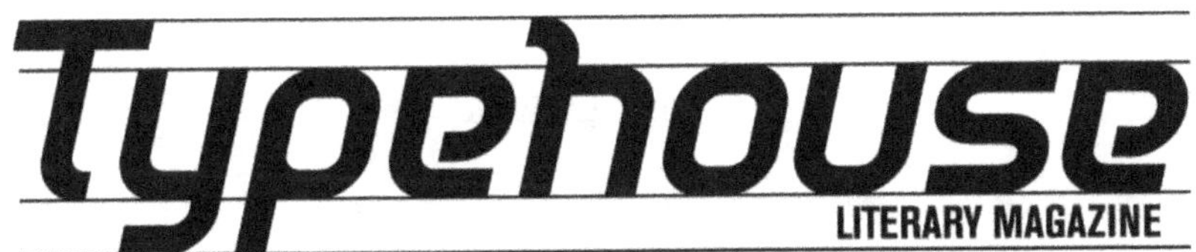

Volume 9, No. 1
Issue 24

Typehouse Literary Magazine

Editor in Chief:
Val Gryphin

Senior Editors:

Mariya Khan (Prose and Poetry)
Yukyan Lam (Prose)
Kameron Ray Morton (Prose)
Alan Perry (Poetry)
Trish Rodriguez (Prose)
Kate Steagall (Prose)
T. E. Wilderson (Prose)

Associate Editors:

Sally Badawi (Prose and Poetry)
Graham Clark (Prose)
Jody Gerbig (Prose)
Emmanuel Ojeikhodion (Poetry)
William Ramsey (Poetry)
Katie Strine (Prose)

Typehouse is a writer-run literary magazine based out of Portland, Oregon. We are always looking for well-crafted, previously unpublished writing and artwork that seeks to capture an awareness of the human condition. To learn more about us, visit our website at www.typehousemagazine.com.

Cover Artwork: **Roast Tea** by Denny E. Marshall
Denny E. Marshall *has had art, poetry, and fiction published. One recent credit is the June 2021 cover of The Society Of Misfit Stories Presents. See more at www.dennymarshall.com.*

Table of Contents

Steve Patterson's *(he/him) photographs have been published in The Sun Magazine, the Portland Oregonian, On the Coast Magazine, the San Pedro Review, the Willamette Weekly, and other regional Pacific Northwest publications. His work has been exhibited in the CoHo Theatre, Common Grounds Coffeehouse, and other independent venues in Portland, Oregon. He also works as a playwright and as an editor.*

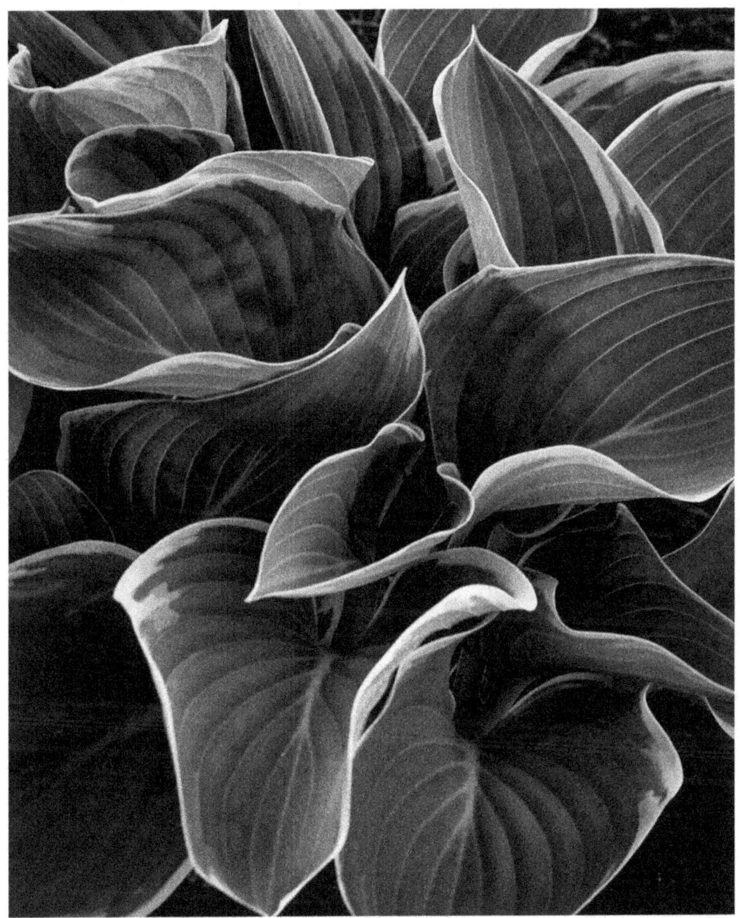

Fabric

In the 1990s, I received a Leica M3 as a gift, and the first satisfying photo I took with it portrayed a hosta in sidelight. Now I grow hostas to photograph them. They conceal mysteries within their shadows, while wearing sumptuous patterned outfits to distract us. Unfurling freshly in spring, they spread their leaves, flower in summer, and slump and decay in autumn. If you can't find life encapsulated in a hosta, keep looking.

Jennifer Bisbing (she/her), best-selling murder mystery author, releases a collection of poems where the reader will find villains still lingering as she fumbles her way through the high desert of Idaho and mountains of Montana. Where the grit softened her. "My life is centered around a secret and covert endeavor: poetry. My father taught the FBI and taught me to see life through a different lens, somehow crime ended up in my poetry." Find her at www.jenniferbisbing.com.

Neon Letters Spell Out Goldie's Diner (minus a burned-out e)

Jennifer Bisbing

The waitress looks
like she should be throwing down whiskey
instead of watered-down coffee in brown mugs
The checkered floor looks shabby—from spur marks, perhaps? Probably
just from the same folks' tired feet,
walking the same way up to the counter,
year after year staying the course
directly to Peggy, who bakes all the homemade pies,
their sweetness wafts through
when the front door swings open

At the closest table—whispers
local gossip or something about the city girl
who just sat down alone in the tattered vinyl booth,
minding her out of town business over eggs and toast

Love sits across the Formica tabletop,
but the seat is empty
If he was there, he'd be wearing his
worn-out overalls
the ones I was always trying to replace
the ones I buried him in
I order his favorite pie,
and only take a fork-full,
he used to protest when I stole it from his slice
Leaving here
means I leave him

Is that why we all stay
in this small town,
the memories wall us in
until leaving means
we have to climb out over everything
and everyone we've collected

I'm too old to lift myself over

Diner Counter (point of view)

The cleaver raises up
Slices through the chicken breast bone
I am two pieces now
The half left when I gave up everything for you
lays listless in this plucked skin
The other half wonders what
wholeness looks like after the blade slid thru
And what will the cook do
with that piece that thumps and flutters

The Writing on the Diner's Bathroom Wall

[Blacked out name] I don't know why
you do anything you do
              I just know my taste buds have dulled
for what you put on my plate

Margery Bayne *(she/her) is a librarian by day and a writer by night from Baltimore, Maryland. She is a published and award-nominated author of speculative and literary short stories, and an aspiring novelist. She has a BA in Creative Writing from Susquehanna University and a Masters of Information and Library Science from the University of Maryland, College Park. For The Writing Cooperative on Medium she writes a biweekly column about short stories called The Short of It. When not reading and writing, she enjoys beating her personal best at running the mile, folding origami bouquets, and being an aunt to four nieces and one nephew. More about her and her writing can be found at www.margerybayne.com, on Medium @margerybayne, and on Twitter @themargerybayne.*

You Make Your Own Luck
Margery Bayne

The witch's cottage was picturesque with its colorful garden and the lace curtains hanging in the windows, but Adelaide was sure it wasn't going to stay that way for long. She shored up her shoulders as she came to stand at the threshold, not knowing what would happen when she identified herself to the person inside. She had her plans, but plans weren't her family's strong suit; that was the downside of being cursed.

Adelaide knocked.

The door opened and in the doorway stood a young woman of Adelaide's equivalent age with almost-black hair down past her shoulders.

Adelaide folded her hands in front of herself. "I'm Adelaide of Longshire, and I'm here to break my family's curse."

The witch rolled her eyes. "My name's Myra. And no."

And thus far the interaction had gone as it had for generations.

"So how are we going to do this?" Myra said. "Do you have a dagger hidden in your boot? Some friends hiding in the trees?"

Adelaide shook her head. "No."

"I heard stories about how one of your lot came after my grandmother with a . . . spear, was it?"

"My uncle." Adelaide had heard the story too. "He slipped on chicken droppings and impaled himself."

Myra raised a pair of thin, uncaring eyebrows. "Did he survive?"

"Yes, actually. Walked with a limp for the rest of his life, but he had a good sense of humor about it. You have to have a good sense of humor about being cursed."

As dry as a summer drought, Myra said, "Do you now?"

Unbothered by the standoff, a chicken clucked its way between their feet.

"Well? Get on with it. I have other things to do with my day."

"That's the thing." Adelaide twisted her folded hands. "I didn't come here to try and kill you."

The witch cocked her head in a tiny, unspoken question.

"It hasn't work in—well—forever. So I thought there ought to be a better way. A less dangerous way. A friendlier way." She cleared her throat. "I entreat to strike a bargain."

"And what do you have to bargain?"

Holding out her palms in all their emptiness, Adelaide said, "I figured I could work the curse off?"

Myra slammed the door in her face.

Adelaide would've had every right to give up then, find accommodations for the night, and start her journey home in the morning. Making this pilgrim-like attempt to break the curse was a more generational rite-of-passage than actual hope. Back home, her family would be pleased she returned uninjured.

However, along with humor, stubbornness was the other factor needed for getting through life cursed with bad luck.

Adelaide camped outside Myra's cottage that night with nothing more than her pack as a pillow. It rained.

#

Adelaide awoke to a blanket being tossed on her face. She drew it back to the sight of heeled boots inches from her nose.

"Come inside for porridge. I can't have an ill wretch on my doorstep. It'll scare away my customers."

Adelaide wrapped the blanket around her damp shoulders and followed Myra inside. She sat where instructed at a sturdy wooden table and accepted the ceramic bowl of porridge with only a mild worry about being poisoned.

The inside of the cottage was done up as elaborately as Myra was done up herself. There was no bare inch to be found with the patterned rugs and wall hangings, plump couches and cushioned stools, as well as all the things one expected to find in a witch's house: dried bundles of herbs hanging from the rafters and shelves of bottles holding mysterious and worrisome contents.

When Myra folded her hands across the table from Adelaide, Adelaide noted the neat crescent moons of her fingernails.

"I've been thinking over your offer."

Adelaide paused with her spoon halfway to her mouth. A drop of the porridge plopped down onto her trousers.

"One lucky thing has happened to you. I'm in need of an assistant. For errands and such."

"Okay."

"It won't be easy."

"Nothing in my life has been easy."

"What I'm saying is . . . " Myra sat up taller in her chair, but it didn't quite manage to intimidate. "I won't take it easy on you."

#

On Monday, Myra sent Adelaide into town with a list of goods to buy. It took Adelaide three trips, a bloody knee, and until nightfall to get them all.

On Tuesday, Myra sent Adelaide into the Ivy Hills to pick potent blue flowers that liked to bloom there this time of spring. Adelaide came back with a bushel full and covered from head to toe with mud.

On Wednesday, Myra sent Adelaide to the well to fetch water. Adelaide fell down the well. It took until noon for another townsfolk to hear her calls from the bottom. While very late and very soaking, she returned to the cottage with her bucket of water anyway.

On Thursday, Myra sent Adelaide up on the cottage roof to clean off the bramble and patch an area Myra had noticed dripping last rain. Adelaide fell off the roof. Twice.

Lucky for her, the one-story cottage didn't have all that high of a roof. Lucky for her, the cottage was surrounded by soft shrubs, grass, and gardens. Lucky for her, the family curse wasn't meant to kill.

She commented on this observed state of things over dinner that evening, a simple stew with bread and cheese.

Myra picked the crust off her slice. "If my ancestor intended to kill yours, they would've just done it. But to cause inconvenience and frustration for years and generations hence . . . that's a lot more rewarding." She flicked the crust into the fire. It wasn't so far into spring yet that the nights could be handled without the hearth lit.

Adelaide knocked her bowl off the table with her elbow, but it didn't crack where it struck the carpeted floor.

"I'm sending you fishing tomorrow," Myra said. "I hope you know how to swim."

#

"You're surprisingly dry," Myra commented when Adelaide returned the next orange-glowed afternoon. She was sitting in the garden on a stool, knitting something lumpy.

"I lost the fishing pole," Adelaide said.

Myra's attention flashed up from her work. She'd lined her gray eyes with smudged kohl, and it made every look sharper. "My fishing pole?"

"Bad luck sometimes catches others in its net."

"I suppose no fish then, either."

Adelaide heaved a net from over her shoulder and plopped the still floppy fish in the dirt at Myra's feet. Myra drew back the toes of her shined boots.

"I didn't lose it in the river."

Adelaide led Myra to the place where the pole was lost, closer to the cottage than not, and pointed up. Myra squinted. High above them in the branches, the fishing pole dangled.

"How did it get up there?"

"I'm not entirely sure. It got caught, and I tugged, and whatever it was caught on tugged back and . . ." Adelaide lifted her arms skyward.

Myra had her long fingers pressed across her lips. And then she laughed. It began like the first drops of rain on your head before the clouds opened up for a storm. And then stormed she did, laughing so hard that she had to grab hold of Adelaide's arm to keep herself standing. Adelaide found herself laughing too.

Myra wiped a tear from the corner of her eye once she regained enough of her breath to speak: "You really do have to find the humor in it."

"It's easy to find it funny when it's the first time it has happened to you."

Although Adelaide hadn't been mad when she said it, Myra found something sour in it nonetheless.

"The only bad luck I've had is waiting around for one of your lot to try and kill me."

There was less humor in the air now.

"Well . . ." Adelaide said when the silence had dragged on too long. "Can't you magic it down?"

Myra eyed the great height over her. "It doesn't work like that."

"What doesn't?"

"Me."

#

Working for Myra and sleeping in the spare closet turned spare bedroom, Adelaide witnessed how a single, young witch made her way in the world. She had daily visitors come to collect potions and poultices, herbs and strange roots, or to sit down over Myra's home-brewed tea to discuss health or love issues and to be prescribed the appropriate remedy. All at a cost, of course. What Adelaide never saw was the same person come twice.

"Don't you get lonely out here?" Adelaide asked with her attempt at mending spread in her lap. The needle's point had become very acquainted with the pad of her thumb.

"I have constant business. How could I get lonely?" Myra didn't look up from her work with a mortar and pestle.

A knock on the door interrupted her and answered the door just a crack, having a perfunctory conversation with whoever was on the other side.

She came back with a bundle of fabric in her arms. "Trade," she muttered to Adelaide on her way to the cabinet.

Once back at the door she passed two vials out to whoever had come knocking, then latched it with a huff.

"What kind of trade?"

Myra shook out the bundle of fabric. It was a coat: woolen, gray, and with a boxy cut. "Not exactly my style, but some people can only pay what they can pay. Are you in need of a coat?"

Adelaide shook her head.

Myra refolded it over her arm. "I'm sure I'll run across someone who needs it by next winter." She tucked the bundle on one of her many shelves.

Adelaide thought of her home, the farm and the farmhouse, and its mass of opponents there and at its nearby neighbors. Her family was large despite its magical disadvantages. They were always bruised and scraped, and getting into scraps and other troubles. But they were surviving, even thriving, bonded together even stronger and more willfully for their misfortunes. The farm was work—farms always were—but it rarely felt like it.

"But don't you do anything for fun?"

Myra dusted her hands off against each other. "Of course I do. You've been here two weeks and think you know my life?"

"All I know is what I've seen," Adelaide said in what she thought was a very measured answer. Myra took it as a challenge.

"I have plenty of fun. I'm even going to a party. Look . . ." She plucked up a letter that had been atop the pile of refuse meant for the hearth. "It's tonight. I hope you have something decent to wear."

"I'm going?" Adelaide plucked her thumb again.

Myra tossed her hair over her shoulder. "Every proper lady arrives with an attendant."

Adelaide wondered when witches had become proper ladies, but she didn't ask. She knew very well that luck wasn't to be tested.

#

Myra scoffed at the sight of her.

Adelaide knew what she looked like, being a bit tallish, with shoulders a bit squarish, and her dusty blonde hair cut short in an unusual fashion, but she held up her chin anyway. "I'm a working woman. Pants are more practical. These are clean and well-mended."

Myra shimmed on a black lace glove. "I suppose it's the best we can do on short notice."

Even on the most regular day, Myra favored petticoats; fabrics embroidered, layered, or laced; and dark colors that contrast-complimented her complexion. So what she wore now looked like what she wore every day, save for the accessories: the jeweled comb in her braided-up hair and a parasol with painted silk panels.

"Was that a courting gift?" Adelaide asked, curious, for the parasol was both a delicate and wondrously constructed thing.

"I can buy my own gifts." She angled the parasol on her shoulder in such a way that blocked Adelaide from her view as they walked side-by-side into town.

At the manor, Myra flicked out her invite to the doorman and brushed inside before she could be announced. Inside, Adelaide saw why Myra intended to burn the invitation. She didn't fit with this company.

To Adelaide's country girl eye, Myra had looked glamorous from the moment she first opened her cottage door. Surrounded by other fancy ladies, something of Myra's glamour dimmed. Her clothes were too dark and old-fashioned. Although the fabrics were expensive—when surrounded by pristine dresses tailored fresh for the season—they revealed their weathering.

From the ogling, standoffish crowds emerged a young gentleman who Adelaide wouldn't call handsome, just well-kept. He extended his arms as he approached.

"Myra. I didn't expect you to come. But it's bad manners to snub the local witch."

Snickering speckled the air.

"Dain," Myra said dryly. "I had to accept one of your invites eventually, or you might think I didn't like you."

In a gesture that increased the giggling, Dain offered an arm. Myra eyed it like it was moldy before she slipped her arm through his. Some unpleasantries were to be endured in a battle of wills.

Myra passed the closed parasol to Adelaide as she was led away. Adelaide stood there, paralyzed between wanting to follow and feeling like she couldn't.

"She realizes that no one wants her here, right?" asked one twitty lady to another. "That the invitation was a joke?"

"Like inviting the help," droned another.

The third, "Well, I'm not going to tell her. I don't want to be cursed."

The parasol started to seem weapon-like.

A hand on her elbow disrupted her murderous notions. A butler motioned her to the edge of the hall, where the other attendants waited—ignored—and ready to spring to required action. He hung the parasol in the closet. Only a few minutes of anxious waiting passed before Adelaide heard raised voices.

She found Myra and Dain arguing on the patio off the back of the hall. Whatever the argument was about, Adelaide didn't know, too distracted by what she saw. Myra trying to brush past Dain in a huff. Dain grabbing her arm to stop her. Myra yanking her arm against his stubborn grip; his grip holding.

"Let go," Myra said through gritted teeth.

Whatever he said in response was a low hiss in her ear. Adelaide didn't need to hear it to march right up to the pair.

"She said 'let go.'"

Dain eyed the length of Adelaide, unimpressed. "Oh look, Myra, you got a new footman."

"You are foul," Myra spat.

Adelaide said, "I really do suggest you let go."

He didn't. Twice was more than enough of a warning. What Adelaide did next might've not been the most proper thing for a fancy party, but it got him to let go.

#

The punch was well-formed. Fingers curled in the correct position to avoid injury, arm cocked at a precise length for leverage, and the aim true. If Adelaide had been a member of any other family, it would've been perfect.

Back at the cottage, Myra cleaned and wrapped Adelaide's knuckles.

"You didn't have to do it." Her now loose hair hid her eyes as she worked, but not enough for Adelaide not to spy their redness.

"I wanted to."

Myra pulled the bandage snug. Adelaide winced.

"I could've taken care of myself. I have ways of taking care of myself."

She held Adelaide's injured hand between her two palms.

Adelaide curled her fingers over Myra's. "People shouldn't always have to take care of themselves all alone."

#

Myra was strange the next day. Quiet, although she would often get quiet when she concentrated on her work. This was a quiet wrapped in a cloak of melancholy.

She spent her afternoon at her worktable, cutting, smashing, and grinding with aggression that worked up a beaded sweat on her brow. For Adelaide's task, she had said, "Just . . . just . . ." then waved a hand in the air, giving up. So Adelaide sat on a stool in a corner where she was least likely to bump or break anything—for it felt like a day for being careful—and just watched Myra move.

After a very decisive chop of the knife into wood, Myra stilled, her hands planted on the table's edge as if it alone was holding her up.

"It does get lonely."

She looked so sad; Adelaide didn't want her to be. All plans of winning her favor—working hard, head down, to the end of the curse—vanished. It was replaced with this: Myra was sad and Adelaide wanted to fix it.

She crossed the room. With a careful touch, she lifted Myra's chin.

Myra stared at her; she blinked. While for Adelaide it had been as gradual as growing dusk; for Myra it was a moment before and after a blink.

Myra pressed onto her tiptoes. That was all that was needed to complete the kiss.

#

Myra ran her fingers through Adelaide's hair. "Why short? It has a nice texture. It would look good long."

"I've learned that long hair is more likely to get into unlucky situations than short."

Myra's mouth turned into a thin, hard line for a moment before she turned away to stir the cauldron simmering in the fireplace.

"What this?" Adelaide asked. Myra had been well into creating the brew when Adelaide awoke. "It smells good." Maybe not to eat, but it had filled the cottage with a refreshing, herby sort of scent.

"It's good for coughs."

"Do people get a lot of coughs in the spring?"

Myra's mouth turned into that line again. "I'm refilling my stock."

Adelaide pressed the tip of her tongue to the back of her teeth. She had a lot of things she wanted to say, but was sure she would tangle any words in the wrong configurations.

From nothing, Myra straightened up. "The parasol."

A leaden weight settled in Adelaide's stomach.

"Did you bring it back from the party?"

Adelaide shook her head.

"Oh, no." Myra hunched over, tangling her fingers in her hair. "No, no, no."

Adelaide reached out a hand for Myra's shoulder and then flitted it away a second later, before contact.

Pacing, Myra started to play out her options. "I can't just go and ask for it back. If Dain knew it was mine, he would toss it into the fire for sure . . ."

"Can you just . . ." Adelaide wiggled her fingers to connote magic.

"It doesn't work like that!"

Myra stopped pacing, but only to stand there in the middle of the cottage, whittling her perfect crescent thumbnail with her teeth.

"I'll do it."

"What?" Myra snapped.

"I'm not so well known in town. I'll sneak in and get it. I left it after all."

"Do you think you can do it?" Myra asked. "Given your . . . condition?"

"I have no idea." But Adelaide had never wanted to succeed at something more in her life.

#

As it was a drizzly day, Adelaide had more than enough reason to keep her hood drawn. Other than soaking her feet in a puddle on the way into town, her trip to the manor went smoothly.

When she reached the gate, the butler from two nights before was crossing the grounds. She called out to him. He curved from his path to meet her.

"Can I help you?" he said in a tone that suggested that she better make it snappy.

Adelaide pulled back her hood in hopes that he would remember her. "Yes. Thank you. And excuse me, but at the party, my lady . . . Myra. You know, the witch . . .?"

The butler stared.

Adelaide gulped. "She left her parasol. I've come to retrieve it, if you wouldn't very much mind."

The butler unlatched the gate. "Follow me."

With each step squelching in the wet grass, he led her around the house to the kitchen entrance. The kitchen was warm and dry, both of which she appreciated, even as he ordered, "Wait here" and left her to the curious looks of the cooks and scullery maids.

The butler returned with an oblong package that seemed the right shape and size for the parasol. "To keep it dry," he explained as he handed it over. He gestured to one of the maids, and she brought Adelaide a basket of loaves still warm from the oven.

"My youngest daughter wouldn't've survived childbirth if it wasn't for your lady. I'll never be able to repay that. If there's ever anything she needs . . ."

"I'll let her know." During her return trek, the drizzle petered out.

#

"My grandmother gave it to me," Myra explained, with the newly returned parasol laid across her knees. She had been near tears at its return, and even closer once hearing what the butler had said. "She was a practical woman. And it was a fanciful gift for a fanciful girl. And my grandmother *got it for me.*" Myra smoothed her hands over the folded silk. "She was all the family I had."

"What of your mother?" Adelaide expected a bad answer.

"She traveled south to Piaya when I was nine and never came back."

"She died?"

"She just didn't come back."

"Your father?"

"I wouldn't know him if I saw him."

No brothers or sisters either, Adelaide could guess. If there were any aunts or uncles or cousins, they weren't important enough to be mentioned.

What a lonely life, living in this cottage with just the memory of all the people that left her.

"Don't look at me like that," Myra said. "Like I'm a tragedy. I'm needed in this town. I help people. Whether they like me or not, I have a profession and purpose here. And if Dain himself showed up tomorrow desperate and ailing, I would help him to the best of my ability, because that's what I do. It's what my grandmother taught me to do."

Adelaide thought if Dain showed up here tomorrow, the first thing she'd do was kick him in the shin and the second thing she'd do was kick him again.

"Makes me wonder," Adelaide asked with a wry grin. "If you'd help Dain tomorrow, what could it have been that my ancestor did that was so bad that his entire family line was cursed."

Myra turned the folded parasol over in her lap once, twice, a third time. She looked up.

"Maybe we could find out."

#

"I'm sure that we both have our own version of the story passed down to us. Probably victimizing our ancestor appropriately and villainizing the other. Perhaps if we compare our stories, we can get a clue to the truth."

Adelaide worried her lip with her teeth. "Are . . . are you sure this will make anything better? Maybe it will make us hate each other."

"While I find you pleasant enough, I need to know if sufficient amends have been made to pardon your whole family." Myra flipped her hair over her shoulder. It was a type of punctuation.

"My story involves my many-great uncle Eustace—"

"Eustace?" Myra laughed. "He had bad luck from the day he was born."

"Eustace was traveling through these parts to get to the city and got injured. He went to the local witch for aid. And the witch, supposedly, had put him under a trance to make him stay and be her servant. When he broke out of the trance and ran away, she cursed him and all his descents with bad luck."

Myra squinted at her. "Is that why you offered to work for me? Is that what you thought I wanted?"

"It might've inspired the idea."

Myra stretched out her legs before her, crossing them at the ankles, the hem of the dress rucked up high enough for Adelaide to spy the delicate curves of her stocking-covered calves.

"My story involves your many-great uncle trying to kidnap the witch's son."

"Very different stories then."

Myra hmmed. "More research then. We have to do more research."

#

What Adelaide thought had been a bench, as it had been draped with a crochet throw and topped with cushions, turned out to be a trunk. Together they dragged it out to the middle of the floor. When Myra unlocked it and threw open the lid, Adelaide saw that it was filled with leather-bound journals.

"What are these?" Adelaide reached out to touch, but paused before her fingers completed their journey.

"Spell books." Myra kneeled before the trunk and plucked one up with no hesitation. "For lack of a better word. Of course, any witch would have plentiful journals in their lifetime, full of scraps, notes, ideas, alterations." She fanned through the pages with her thumb. The old, yellowed pages crinkled. "These are the final product. A compendium of each's best knowledge, of spell or potion, discovered or amended."

"And what're we doing with them?" Adelaide asked.

"What one does with books. Read them."

"And to what purpose are we reading them?"

Myra snapped the book in her hand shut. "To find the one with the bad luck spell, of course."

"Of course," Adelaide repeated, not feeling "of course" at all. "You don't know which one has it in it?"

"Believe it or not, your family's bad luck curse is not the center of my daily interests."

"So we're reading all these?" Adelaide knew how to read, but didn't do much for pleasure after she outgrew the fairy stories of her youth.

"Yes." Myra laid a journal open on her lap. "You see, a spell book isn't just like a list of recipes . . . ingredients, and rituals, that is. Each spell has a story. Inspiration and motivation behind it. And that bad luck spell surely will have the story."

"Your sides' story."

"Sure, but untainted by generations of hand-me-down tales. A little closer to the truth. And . . . the counter-curse."

#

Adelaide rubbed at her tired eyes as she set a spell book into the discard pile.

"All I know for sure," Myra said as she snapped another journal closed, "Is the only thing that definitely won't break the curse is one of your lot killing me. If one of you managed it'd probably just make it worse. A natural contingency built into many a curse. I know that's something you'd expect to hear from someone in my position, but I think you know me well enough now to believe it."

"If it's any salve," Adelaide said. "I don't think any of my family wants to kill you. It's more of a tradition to try than an actual belief it will work."

"What a tradition," Myra remarked dryly.

A knock on the door interrupted.

Myra sighed. "They all have to show up today when I'm busy after avoiding me since the party."

"Avoiding you?"

"Word of Dain and our fight had to travel. His family does a lot of business in this town. They couldn't look to be choosing my side." She raked her fingers through her hair, working out a few tangles. "I may save their lives and marriages and complexions, but he gives them money."

The knock repeated.

"Coming!"

This guest—a middle-aged and frazzled woman—had to be invited in and have tea offered.

"It's just not an easy thing to talk about," she prefaced, fingers twitchy on a chintzy teacup. None of Myra's dishware matched, but it was all eccentric and beautiful.

"Please, Mrs. Dower, take your time." Myra laid a calming hand on top of the woman's, but her eyes kept sliding back to the trunk of spell books spilled out on the floor.

The teacup clattered as Mrs. Dower replaced it onto the saucer. "I need you to understand, I love my children."

"Of course," Myra said.

"And my husband."

"Brava on the success of your marriage."

"And I also love . . ." Mrs. Dower went rather pink. "Being close to my husband."

"Again, brava on the success of your marriage."

Then it exploded out of the woman: "But I just can't have any more babies."

"See?" Myra said. "Wasn't that easy?"

She sent Mrs. Dowers off with a potion, instructions, orders to come back next month for resupply, and an insistence that this one was on the house.

After the thankful woman had been urged out the door, Myra collapsed in the chair—just like her teacups, mismatched and exquisite—that Adelaide had noticed she favored.

"She didn't have to make it such an ordeal. We all know what happens in the marriage bedroom."

Adelaide felt herself growing heated around the face.

Myra noticed. Myra laughed. "Have I offended your farm girl sensibilities, Ada?"

Adelaide grew hotter, because 'Ada.' No one called her that save for her mother and kid brother, a sort of offhand nickname that was familiar as it was affectionate.

"Well . . ." Myra slid like water from the chair back to the floor. "Back to work."

#

"It's not here!" Myra thumped down the last of the journals on the floor. "How could it not be here?"

It had taken them into the night and, after a rest, into the next morning to finish their search of the spell books. Adelaide's eyes ached in a way she didn't know eyes could ache.

Grinding her fingers into those very aching eyes, she asked, "Could you've missed something?"

They hadn't been reading the journals to detailed completion, but skimming over the contents—disordered and unlabeled—to find the spell they were searching for.

"I don't know," Myra snarled. "Could *you* have missed something?"

Adelaide leaned away. "I've tried my best."

Myra threw up her hands. "Your best? Your best is a mess."

It felt cruel of her to say it, like a hot weight in Adelaide's gut. She knew a good deal of her life was a mess, but she tried and . . .

"It's not my fault."

Myra stood and started pacing in front of the hearth, dragging her hands through her hair and over her face. Within all the pacing, frantic and exhausted, words escaped her:

"I thought if I found it, I'd have a clue what to do. That maybe there would be an easy fix. A contingency. Or I could take it to a real witch, at least."

"Stop." Adelaide pressed up onto her knees. "Stop." She got to her feet. She didn't care for seeing Myra like this.

Myra stopped pacing, but didn't calm. Hands fisted in the hair at the nape of her neck, she said, "I'm a horrible person. Awful."

Adelaide stepped forward. "You're not."

Myra stepped backward. "I am. I—I don't know how to break the curse. I never have. I'm not even magic."

The confession thudded inside the cottage as if it had been thundering.

"But . . ." The potions. The spell books. The fact that everyone called her a witch.

"It sometimes skips a generation. My grandmother was, but . . . I'm just a herbalist. I do my best with what I can, but if generations of people are used to this being the witch's cottage . . ." She dropped her arms, her eyes glossy. "I'm sorry."

Adelaide didn't know what to say. Or feel. All her plans to save her family . . . But hadn't she lost track of her plans a long time ago?

Myra made her final confession: "If I could break the curse for you, I would."

Adelaide said, "I need to think."

#

With summer approaching, the night air was pleasant and the cricket song strong. The forest wasn't a silent entity, just wordless. That was what Adelaide needed right now, no words so that her thoughts and feelings had a place to stretch themselves out. She felt betrayed, somewhat, because Myra and herself had made an agreement. An exchange. Sure, it had been flimsy terms, Adelaide hoping to appeal to her favor and knowing it more likely than not to fail. But she had been operating on a slim hope. A hope that never existed.

On the other hand, Myra was really contrite over the matter. She hadn't needed to admit her deficiency with magic at all. And it seemed she had been trying her best to find a way out of the curse.

Wasn't it better to have a non-witch who wanted to break the curse than a witch who could do it full well and just refused?

Was it?

Adelaide slept outside that night, the first time since her first day. Tonight, it was that perfect temperature between cool and warm that one got on rare days in the transitioning seasons. Despite everything else, it was a lucky night to be mad.

#

When Adelaide returned in the morning, Myra was wearing the same frock as the day before.

"I'm not mad," Adelaide said, and she wasn't. What she was: Refreshed from a heavy sleep in the night air, and resigned. "But this means I have to go home."

Myra nodded, tightly. "Let me pack you some food. And some . . . I have all that cough remedy brewed, so . . . It's the least I can do."

Adelaide agreed but remained sitting outside where the chickens clucked. While she wasn't mad, she was heavy. The idea of taking on the first of several days' long walk back home was unappealing, even as appealing as the lure of home was.

Plus, she was afraid to go back inside the cottage. To be overwhelmed by the smells of herbs, tea, and perfume. Afraid she would miss the feel of the velvet cushions, the look of mismatched decorations, and the woman that governed over all of them.

They hadn't spoken of the kiss since it happened. They hadn't kissed again. While the surrounding air had grown more at ease after, Myra freer with soft touches and softer laughter, Adelaide had assumed that Myra hadn't wanted to repeat the experience but also hadn't wanted to embarrass Adelaide by bringing it up.

Myra returned outside with Adelaide's pack, properly stuffed.

"Do you mean to leave right away?"

"I suppose," Adelaide said.

Ask me to stay, she thought, as if she, mundane as could be, could magic the thought into Myra's head. Ask me to stay. She couldn't stay without reason, but if Myra asked . . .

Myra took in a breath that sounded suspiciously like a sniffle.

"Travel safe. Promise?"

Adelaide nodded. That's all she could manage.

She adjusted the straps of her pack, hoping it was a delay that would escalate into another delay. It didn't. Never in her life had Adelaide been lucky enough to get what she wanted.

Aligning herself in the direction of the eastward path, she started away.

"Eh! Lady! Lady!" A young errand boy from town was running up the path from the village. It was nothing Adelaide had to deal with now.

His pounding feet ran straight past Myra's cottage and towards Adelaide.

"I'm talking to you, lady!" He skidded to a stop where Adelaide paused. He held out a folded piece of parchment. "You got a letter."

The scrawl on the front was her mother's.

"Were you leaving?" the boy asked. "Lucky getting here just in time, eh?"

Myra paid the boy, and he ran off back to town.

Adelaide had written home once during her stay, just reassurances she had arrived safely, that the witch hadn't killed her on sight, and that she didn't know how long she would be.

"Were you expecting a letter?" Myra asked.

Adelaide shook her head.

"Then you did get it just in time. How fortuitous."

"Fortuitous." Adelaide flipped the letter over and broke the wax.

Dearest Adelaide,

My wonderful and resourceful daughter, whatever you've done has worked! I didn't notice at first. None of us did.

Last week, when your father was patching the roof, he lost his balance on the ladder and looked like he was going to fall, but he caught himself at the last moment. He clung to the rungs waiting for the ladder to topple anyway, the shingles to slide off, lightning to strike—anything!—and it didn't. Neither of us knew what to think, but we started paying attention.

It's been like that for the whole family. All the little things that used to go wrong aren't. Of course, there are still some scraped knees

"What is it?" Myra demanded. "You look pale."

Adelaide passed over the letter. Soon she heard Myra sucking in a breath, coming to the same conclusion.

Adelaide didn't leave that morning.

\#

"Now that I think about it . . . things have been going rather smoothly lately." Adelaide wasn't sure the last time she tripped or spilled soup on her pants. "The last time I hurt myself was . . ." She held up the hand she had punched Dain with. "And everything went awfully easy when I went to get your parasol, and that was a situation rife with unlucky possibilities"

"So whatever broke the curse had to have happened between . . ." Myra trailed off.

Only one thing of note had occurred between those events, and even though she didn't say it, she could feel it through the flushed heat climbing up her neck.

Myra laughed in an airy way that was reminiscent of hysteria. "A kiss? How trite. A kiss is too easy of a thing to hang a curse on."

Adelaide hadn't thought the kiss had been easy when she had given it; she thought even less so now.

"Look at all these spell books lying about." Myra swooped down to collect one she had left tossed in a far corner, then to the trunk; she reached inside. Her hand retreated with a jerk.

"What's wrong?" Adelaide leaned to see.

"This trunk has a false bottom."

Adelaide helped her pry it out. Under it was one last journal.

\#

They sat shoulder-to-shoulder on the floor to read it together. This one was an actual journal instead of a spell book, the passages recorded day by day, written by the hand of Myra's many-great grandfather—son of a witch, magic in his own right, still in the apprentice stages—who fell in love with a traveler, Adelaide's many-great uncle.

"Uncle Eustace wasn't enchanted. He was just in love," Adelaide said when they were partway through.

"And there was no kidnapping attempt," Myra said, a few pages later. "They were trying to run away together."

But there was more to the story than that. Their two families didn't want them together. Because of old fears about witches and outsiders and other backward things. Two families that forced them apart.

So Myra's many-great grandfather, heartbroken, sent his vengeance through a curse.

Adelaide pointed at the page. "Is that a squiggle or an 's'?"

"I believe an 's.'"

"But then . . . curse*s*. More than one."

Myra pulled the journal close and started reading faster. She turned the page, read some more, then sucked in a breath.

Before Adelaide could ask what, she started aloud: "To Eustace's family, may they forever be ill-favored by luck in all of their ventures, so they can never forget what they have broken. To my own family, may they forever be alone, so they will always know what they've done to me. These are both bound until a time when there is reconciliation in equal amount to what was taken from us."

Adelaide wasn't sure exactly what that all meant in its practicalities. Maybe Myra, a non-witch but raised by one, knew. What Adelaide thought she understood was that it was more than a kiss between them that had broken the curses; it was a scary and thrilling thought.

Myra dropped the journal. It fell open-faced on the floor. "I want you to stay. I could use a hand around here. I could teach you everything I know, and we could work together, or you could do something else in town. Whatever you wanted, I'd help you." After catching her breath, she added, "It's a selfish want, I know, but I want it. I'd miss you too much if you go."

The offer that Adelaide had ached for just this morning hung there. A reason to stay a little longer. This was a reason to stay a lot longer. But her family needed her; they needed all the help they could get on the farm, as neither planting nor growing nor harvesting went smoothly under their cursed hands and . . . Oh, right.

Wasn't it also true that a time came for all young people to leave their childhood home and begin to make a life of their own?

"I have to go back," Adelaide said. "To visit. And to get the rest of my things, so I can move in proper."

Myra tackle-hugged her, Adelaide catching her as firmly in her arms as Myra had flung them around her shoulders. Her face was full of Myra's hair, and she couldn't quite breathe, but she never wanted to let go.

#

Myra entwined her fingers with Adelaide's as she experimented with hand-holding.

"Did you know whatever happened to your uncle Eustace?"

"Grew old as a bachelor. Went off on a walk one day, and was so unlucky he got so lost that he never came back," Adelaide said. "Or that's the story. And yours?"

"Moved out to make his own way. Traveled west. Never came back after that."

"Do you—" She started, then shook her head. "Never mind."

"What was it?"

"It's stupid."

"I do not believe you think stupid thoughts."

Adelaide lifted their entangled hands and pressed a kiss on Myra's knuckles. For all the times she had made Adelaide heat up, it was now her turn. Myra went a fetching shade of pink that clashed with her dark plum bodice.

"Do you think they maybe found each other? Years later? After they left?"

Myra laid her head on Adelaide's shoulder.

"I hope so. It's an unlucky thing to be alone."

Laramie Wyoming (she/her) is an emerging author from New York City. Her short story "The Flower Wars" will be published in Wolfsinger Publishing's upcoming Us/Them anthology. She is going to attend Oberlin College, where she plans on majoring in archaeology.

My Sister, Elenore
Laramie Wyoming

My sister was very pretty. All the boys, and a lot of the girls, would watch her when we walked into church, even in those awful clothes she wore. Ma sewed them for her, I think intentionally to disfigure and lump-ify her; my parents together agreed that boys should not be looking at Elenore. But they did, anyways, and I would scowl at them, turning my head as we sat down in a pew, so I could scowl at them all. I didn't want my sister getting in trouble, and, though I didn't realize it until I was in middle school, I was jealous of her, too—I was ugly enough to choose my own outfits on Sunday. It wasn't her fault that she looked like that, and despite what magazines and movies told us, being pretty did her no good.

During church, I would look at her, mostly, especially when I was younger and didn't have school friends to sit behind. She must've been about fifteen then, making me seven.

Back then, she still did her hair up in curlers every night, so that it molded in ringlets and waves. It was similar to a print I saw of a fashionable lady in a book from 1840 or so. But nobody else did their hair like that for at least a hundred years, except my sister, who was the only one in the world it could look good on.

She had let me use her curlers, too. One morning I came in for breakfast with my whole head hived up in curlers, which Ma promptly unpinned, saying "Absolutely not." I could feel the curls falling around my face, smooth and glossy—not frizzy like my hair normally felt. Ma pushed her fingers through the top of my scalp. "You look like a poodle, Genevieve," she scowled, then turned to my sister. "She's too young for this, Elenore. She looks ridiculous."

When I saw myself in the mirror, I had to agree—I didn't look too good. I pulled it up in a ponytail and left one curl hanging out in the front, which I thought made me look like a storybook character—the free-spirited, princess kind that can charm animals. Of course, in New York, all we had were pigeons, and there weren't many obvious routes to gallantry and magic. At least, there weren't any that I saw clearly. Maybe on Fifth Avenue, on the

East Side, but not where we were downtown. I thought it was probably the barest, greyest part of Manhattan.

Yet I was always practicing my most graceful walk when I went down the street to school, and I continued having my sister curl just the front piece of my hair, which I could hide from Ma but let out at school. Elenore must have known that I looked absurd like that, but I liked it, so she let it be. I don't know why our parents let Elenore curl hers. By my own principal, I always wore my hair entirely flat to church.

The candlelight in church, I thought, made Elenore look sick, like she had a fever, and not in the pretty, pink-cheeked, storybook fever. Her curls were jet black, but she had used bleach to turn one piece near the front an orangey-blonde color. She'd been grounded a week for doing that.

Elenore's eyes were dark, too, and they were shifty under her long lashes; she was always watching people from behind their curtains. What added the most to her beauty was a pair of scars: one down the center of her nose, and a long one across her cheek. I didn't know the story of the long one; nobody would ever tell me when I asked, and it put them in such a bad mood, I understood it was something that would never be talked about and stopped asking.

The nose scar was something I had witnessed. The cat, George, had been asleep in bed with Elenore. We shared a bedroom, and I was awake when our dad came into the room to get George; he was going to bed and wanted to sleep with him. So our dad reached down to get the cat from beside my sister, and George didn't want to go; our dad was tugging at him by the hips. The cat started scratching out, and one of his claws ended up deep in the bridge of my sister's nose, and as he was dragged backwards, his claw was dragged down her face. The cut was so deep, she told me later, that she hadn't even felt the pain. It was a spreading heat over her face that told her something was wrong. When she brought a hand to it, she felt it was slick with blood. She went to the bathroom, put some wadded-up toilet paper on it, and went back to bed.

The second scar showed up after she had been away for three days, staying, supposedly, with her friend Anne. My mom threw a fit when Elenore came home with that. She threw an even bigger fit when my sister refused to tell her what had happened. She yelled at Elenore, she beat Elenore, but still she wouldn't say, she just screamed back and cried after she'd had her hair yanked so hard she fell to the floor. I asked her quietly, at night (she went to bed later than me, but I couldn't fall asleep with all the screaming they were doing, anyways). She still wouldn't say. In fact, she was mad. "None of your fucking business." I apologized, and she said "Just shut up." I did.

She never tried to cover up the scars, which she could've done, with her hair combed to the side. At least, she would have covered the one on her cheek.

Around that time, I read about families a lot. I read about Darry, Sodapop, and Ponyboy in *The Outsiders*, and the Glass family in J. D. Salinger's books. My favorite was *Little Women*. None of the families I read about were like mine, and even though I sought that out, it made me sad. I had never expected very much of my parents, which is probably hard to believe from a Freudian perspective, but it is true. I expected more of my sister. In the books, older siblings were so nice. They lavished love on the little ones, they helped them with homework, they gave them pet names and worldly advice, and in return, they were deified and beloved. And I did love my sister, and she loved me. But she wasn't patient, she wasn't nurturing or tender-hearted. Her temper was so short, and she was selfish with her time, a lot of which she spent writing.

I read her diaries (which I didn't think was morally wrong), and that is how I learned that she loved me. She had written two things that proved it.

The first was that she was glad she was born first, and that Ma had chosen to hate her instead of me. She said she knew that she was strong enough to take it and she would be getting out sooner because she was older.

The second thing she wrote was that on the subway one night, she had seen what I could only assume was a monster. She said he was disguised as a shadowy man, with cracked fingers, each a foot long; with hunched, knotted shoulders; wild white eyes. She'd seen him on the opposite end of the car, coming towards her. It was late at night; nobody else was there but the two of them. She couldn't move her body, she just screamed and screamed. When the doors opened with their familiar ding, she was broken from the spell—she jumped up and ran from the car, into the station, still screaming. The monster was carried away, but she still didn't feel safe. As each car passed, on all the other trains that came by, she saw no monster, but she couldn't trust that it wasn't there.

At that time, she'd been most seriously dating a boy named Neil, and this is what she said in her diary, more or less: "I kept thinking, with each passing car, what if Neil is dead in there? What if that monster killed Neal, too? And it hardly phased me, even. I pictured Genevieve, though, Dad, and even mom, and I thought I would give ten Neils up any time of day to save one of them."

This was a lot for my sister to say, because she really, really loved her boyfriends. If someone put a hand on her when they shouldn't, she'd turn around and smack them (she told me this at night, when we were in bed, and advised me to do the same if someone ever did that to me. She said I could also verbally abuse them until they cried). But when a boy treated her well, she was kind—more than, really. She always had at least three boyfriends, some of whom would walk her to school in the morning, or, really, walk us, and then there would be one to walk her home from school, and another waiting to see if she could sneak out that night, or go out once her homework was done and Ma was in a good enough mood.

If my mother knew Elenore had boyfriends, she would've just shat herself. She would've had a heart attack and *died*, though, if she knew what Elenore *did* with those boys.

I never saw them more than kiss one night, while I was watching from the window. She had snuck out that time. He was a boy from school—Kurt—and while they kissed, she pulled away from him to play with his hair, which was this nice, sandy blonde. She was smiling the whole time, a real, serious smile. She put a hand on his chest—he was wearing a plain white t-shirt—and he hugged her to him. Since I was her sister, I was a little grossed out, a little jealous, and pretty impressed. It was the most romantic thing I'd ever seen in real life. It was even more so when she turned to go into our building, and he began walking away, then turned back around, grabbed her by the hand, and kissed her once more. You could tell he needed her, and that made me smile despite any inherent grossness or jealousy. I liked, too, how he walked away, with his hands in his pockets, turning his head even after he knew she'd left.

When Elenore came back up to our room that night, I was already in bed, pretending to be asleep. I saw her go over to the window, and I knew he'd already gone around the corner. I wanted to tell her, "He really likes you, he kept looking back." But she would've been mad at me for spying, and she probably already knew all I had to say, anyways.

She would tell me about some of the boys, especially the ones she really liked. But it was from other girls that I learned what she did with them.

I was a freshman when she was a senior in high school, and the girls in my grade and the grades above me would tell me the names she was called.

"Your sister's the slut of the school, the biggest whore, she'll put out for anyone."

One boy cornered me in the bathroom. "You do what your sister does?"

I shoved him away. I said "No," as firmly as I could.

"You should be thanking me for coming up to you. You're too ugly to say no." Thus my shame was doubled.

Not knowing what else to say, I cried desperately, "Go talk to Elenore, then!"

"That used-up skank?"

I slapped him across the face, and he had the audacity to report me to the principal. I refused to explain why I had done it; I got in-school suspension for a week, and beat at home, because I wouldn't tell Ma, or my dad, or Elenore, why I had thought it was okay to slap someone.

Then there was Jerry, the one Elenore loved the most. He didn't go to school with us; he was two years older than her. He worked at the deli counter at the supermarket on our corner. I rarely went there, so I didn't know who

Jerry was when she mentioned him to me. I teased her because I thought he had a funny name. This, Elenore didn't like. "He's so nice, I swear, you'd like him," she told me. To prove it, she took me for a cold cut sandwich one day after school. We went into the old supermarket. The isles were dark, because they were blocked from the windows. The walking space between shelves of canned soup and powdered eggs was so narrow, you had to go single file. It was a labyrinth of wire racks and concrete pillars, and my sister deftly wove her way through; at the end of the maze was Jerry, at the deli counter, which was up against a wall.

"Jerry, this is my sister, Genevieve."

Jerry looked up. "Hey Genevieve, hey Elenore." He wasn't particularly handsome, but he wasn't bad to look at, either. He had dark hair; he had a nice smile.

"Hello," I said.

"You guys want some sandwiches?" he asked, almost shyly, which made me wonder if it was my presence that was upsetting his balance.

He gave us sandwiches with whatever we wanted. "On me," he said when I asked Elenore to pay, because I had no money.

I wish I could say something more consequential about Jerry, but he didn't strike me as exceptionally cool, tough or intelligent. I guess he seemed nice enough.

"We don't see him at church," I said as we walked out.

"He's Jewish," my sister said. "Are you gonna eat that?"

"So could you marry him? Hypothetically, of course."

"Yes. Are you gonna eat that?"

"No," I said, and gave her my sandwich; I don't like cold cuts. She ate it, but didn't explain any more as to what was so fantastic about Jerry, and I didn't ask.

She told us on Easter, when we went to Central Park for a picnic. It was only our family of four; we were basically estranged from our relatives on either side. Holidays were more depressing than fun for me and Elenore after we realized that other people, even the religious ones, did festive things.

That year, I remember, Elenore had asked to bring one of her friends along, a girl named Judy. Our parents had said no.

So she told us without Judy there that she was pregnant. Ma wasn't angry at first, she just clasped a hand over her mouth and made a face as though she were witnessing a crime against humanity. That annoyed me.

She turned to rage later, but Elenore was already gone by then. She'd gone to live with the father, who I knew was Jerry. I was no longer allowed to leave the house, except for going to and from school. She screamed that my sister was a threat to herself and others, others meaning us, especially.

"What do you think she's doing, hiding in an alley to stab me if I go to the library?" I screamed, in tears, when she insisted I couldn't go and return an overdue book.

"I don't know!" Ma screamed back. "I have no idea where she is, and she's clearly not in a stable condition!"

The morning after Easter, I went to school late. I stopped by Jerry's deli counter. He was there, he looked up when he saw me. "Hey, Genevieve."

"Is my sister with you?"

He nodded. "You wanna see her?"

"Yes. What's the address?" He turned and walked out from behind the counter.

"Follow me," he said, and I was suddenly afraid of him. What had he done to my sister, and what would he do to me?" I was very afraid of rape at that point in my life.

It turned out that there was a small apartment attached to the grocery. This was where my sister was living, in one room with a small floor mattress and a naked lightbulb and all of Elenore's familiar clothes.

She was reading a magazine and jumped when we opened the door. You could see she'd been crying, which made sense. She looked up at Jerry, who nodded and ducked out of the room.

"Genevieve," she said, "How's Ma?"

"Awful," I whispered, and Elenore's eyes began to tear.

"She hasn't been beating you over it, has she?"

"No," I lied.

"She can't know about here, or Jerry, or anything."

"I know," I said. And then, because I still wanted a kind, storybook family, I said "Whaddya think I am, stoopit?" in my best Robert DeNiro impression. It was a thing we sometimes did. Elenore laughed and sniffled.

"Don't come by too often, I don't want you getting in trouble. Or getting me in trouble."

"Okay. How long will you be here for?"

"I don't know."

"Okay." There was a pause. "Do you want me to bring you your allowance—my allowance money?"

"No, that's alright, Genevieve. Now go, don't miss school."

She was right: the school would let your parents know if you were late too often. So I went.

On the nights my dad was home, I got no sleep. Ma never stopped yelling at him; I could hear it through the walls. She said the same things over and over. Nobody has hurt me so badly in my life. How did I raise such a whore. Why does she hate me? She did it just to spite me. I'm going to call the police. That one she threatened a lot, but she never did.

On the nights my dad wasn't home, I was kept up by Ma's wailing and crying. In my mind, she was doing it all for dramatic effect, but I guess she was in pain.

She beat me when she wasn't walking around crying and beating herself, which gave her black-and-blue temples and clumps of missing hair.

I cried a lot, too, at home and even at school, a thing I hadn't done since I was about five years old. I didn't go to the cafeteria for lunch; I walked around the hallways when they were empty, crying very quietly. That also happened to be the first time a boy liked me: Jack, who was in my grade, was also in the hallway during lunch, doing homework that was due next period. He saw me crying and pulled me aside, talked to me. He was one of the boys that every girl liked, because he was nice, flirted with them all very suavely, and was very good-looking. He asked me what was wrong, and I didn't know what to tell him. "Things are just really hard at home right now."

I had always sort of dreamed of a boy coming to save me and comfort me, but now that one was trying to, I changed my mind.

#

I saw Elenore again a month later. I looked for signs of pregnancy, but she was still thin.

"I spend half my time here and half my time at Jerrys'."

"Why not all the time at Jerrys'?"

"Don't be obnoxious. His parents live with him." I took this as a nice way of saying "He lives with his parents."

I pouted. "I'm not being obnoxious." There was a moment of silence, and then I asked, with my heart beating faster, because it was a scary question to ask, we didn't ask questions like this in our family: "Do you love him?"

She just shrugged. "I'm moving soon. When Judy graduates, she and I are going to live together."

"Okay… how will I know? When you leave and how to find you?"

She sat for a moment, thinking. "Jerry will give you the address."

"But how will I know when you've left, when to get it from him?"

"Um." She shrugged again.

I bit my lip. "How about… like Troy, the battle? You know?"

"Of course I don't know. What's Troy?" she said it rather disinterested.

"There was a light on the mountain, so that everybody knew that the war was done."

"Oh."

"So before you leave, the night before, leave your light on, and I'll see it from across the street, I'll know."

"Okay. And when I move, you can always come, if you need."

"Thanks." She bit her lip. "You know what?" she said, and I could tell she was nervous, too, her heart was also pounding, "What if we both leave our lights on every night, and the night mine are off, I'm gone. I'll even leave them on while I'm at Jerry's."

"Okay." I was touched: it was her way of saying that she missed me, that she loved me.

And we did it. Ma thought I kept my light on at night because I'd gone nervous and pathological, from kids bullying me at school over my sister being pregnant. She wanted me to switch schools, she wanted to move. She talked incessantly about moving to the West Village, a neighborhood we could never afford and never fit into. I don't know where she got the idea.

Almost exactly eight months after we'd spoken, my sister's light went out.

That was about the same time that I finished reading Lolita, a book that my classmates had glorified to me. I guess they thought it gave us 14-year-old girls some womanly, sexed-up place in the world, but I hated it. I didn't think it was exciting, erotic, taboo, or anything. I thought it was only sad, despicable, sad. I imagined my sister like Lolita at the end of the book, living in some house in the middle of nowhere, with a dope of a husband; sad and wounded, in a sort of shambles, pitiable, her beauty gone, hopeless…

I didn't want her to seem that way, but she did.

I thought about Elenore only when it would be impossible to reach her—she'd slip into my mind as I was taking a test, while I was at the dinner table, while my friend was talking to me in the hallway. But of course, she was always there, in my pocket or on my shoulder; it was just when she chose to make herself known.

It was a while before I allowed myself to think of her clearly as I walked home. But eventually, it did happen; I got the address from Jerry, and I wrote letters to Elenore, which I sent to her address. I would visit, but I was afraid.

I wrote every night after dinner, and after that, I fell asleep with my light on.

Traci McMickle *(she/her) is a bi/pan/queer poet from Montana where she lives with a spouse and an incorrigible Rottweiler. She has an MFA from the University of New Orleans and currently manages social media for Hot Redhead Media, a small press.*

What I Heard You Say

Traci McMickle

A Golden Shovel of "This is Just to Say" by William Carlos Williams

I cower in the shadow of the day our *we* becomes *I*,
when all our tenses turn, when *have*
is eaten
down to a hard and wrinkled *had* — the
last stone left when all the plums
are gone. Is that
what you were
trying to tell me, standing in
the kitchen that day, your voice lower than the
rumble of the icebox?

That someday you'd be gone and
I'd be left to wonder which
of my words were the last ones you
would remember? We were
talking about something mundane, probably.
Like how we should be saving
more money for
big things instead of wasting it going out to breakfast.

Would you forgive
me if I went first? Or would you remember me
with the bitterness of apples picked before they
turned ripe? Kaleidoscoped in morning light, were
you musing on how everything delicious
eventually turns so
rotten? *Eat things while they're sweet,*
you told me, and
even though you said it so
lightly, my teeth chattered with cold.

A fan of all things fantastical and frightening, **Shannon Lawrence** *writes primarily horror and fantasy. Her stories can be found in over forty anthologies and magazines, and her three solo horror short story collections,* <u>Blue Sludge Blues & Other Abominations,</u> <u>Bruised Souls & Other Torments,</u> *and* <u>Happy Ghoulidays</u> *are available now. You can also find her as a co-host of the podcast "Mysteries, Monsters, & Mayhem." When she's not writing, she's hiking through the wilds of Colorado and photographing her magnificent surroundings, where, coincidentally, there's always a place to hide a body or birth a monster. Find her at www.thewarriormuse.com.*

Coffin Birth
Shannon Lawrence

The sound of her own blood pulsing inside her ears slows, becomes sluggish.

Her senses dull. The sights blur, the sounds mute, the smells fade. Even the pains lashing her body pull away, becoming background sensations. The taste of her own blood in her mouth, strong, almost unbearable before, sweetens and mellows, floating over her tongue.

She can no longer hear the voices, the raucous cries, the hateful words.

A sensation of weightlessness comes over her. She's gliding, sliding through the air. When she tries to open her eyes, the lashes are gummed together. Cracks of yellow light seep through, but the landscape is invisible. Briefly, a face floats into view. A fleshy blob with no discerning features except for the yawning darkness of a mouth.

Then the baby moves, a rolling flutter at her center, and she remembers why she fought so hard, who she was fighting for.

Her senses come crashing back. All at once it's too much. Agony, terror, sensory overload. The voices are quieter now than they were before. Gruff and low, arguing, panicking. The words they used before—squaw, trash, redskin, whore—have changed now to "the body," "this bitch," and "what do we do?" Anger and hatred to fear and paranoia.

Their hands are rough on her body as they carry her, drop her into the back of a pickup truck, the bed hard and rippling, hurting. A metallic rasp is followed by the slam of the pickup's gate.

Cold. Everything is frigid, from the air to the metal she lies on. It smells of soil, manure, metal. The baby moves again, restless, hungry. Suffocating. He rolls and kicks. Inside his mother, he fights.

Because she has stopped.

Her breath feels like syrup in her lungs. All she wants is to fall asleep, to give into the dark edges that creep in on her.

"Shhh," she whispers, lifting a hand that feels heavy like cement to place it on her roiling belly. "Shhh," she says again. Warm liquid spills onto her lips, her chin, and then she feels nothing.

#

Upon waking, Rainey feels nothing. No pain, nothing. A person always feels something, like the surface on which they rest or the ambient temperature of the room. She exists in a vacuum of sensation. She attempts to move her hand, but can't tell if anything happens. All is dark, but she can't feel if her eyes are open or closed. The absence of sound, taste, and smell scares her. At least that can be "felt." Even as her fear swells, the comfort of having an emotion calms her. Somehow she perceives both things at once.

Just as she cannot put hands to her belly or discern movement, she senses her baby boy's presence. He's here with her, wherever here is.

Rainey tries to remember what led her here. At first, it's hazy, but the harder she concentrates, the more it comes back to her. At first there's a single voice. She can't quite make out what it says, but she can tell it's a man's voice. It's a higher male voice, more of a tenor than a bass. She ignored it at first, but now she focuses on it, here deep inside her head. He's yelling and laughing, encouraging shouts coming from other male voices.

"Hey there, pretty lady, why don't you come hang out with a real man."

He's behind her, so maybe he can't see her swollen belly from this angle. She keeps walking, hoping he'll take the hint or get bored, leave her alone.

He does neither, though. His voice gets louder, clearer, as he trails her. For now, his friends stay back. His footsteps crunch on the gravel and the scent of cigarette smoke catches up to Rainey.

She speeds up, takes out her phone. The screen pops on, bright in the low light of late evening, and she glances down long enough to enter her password and pull up the recent calls. Here, she selects her boyfriend's name, Stephen, and waits, the phone now to her ear. The ring tone is low, not loud enough to drown out the man's voice.

"Hey, squaw. I'm offering you an opportunity to try white meat. Bet you'll never go back to those long-haired savages you're used to."

The aggression in his voice is ramping up the longer this goes on. Rainey doesn't know what to do. The strip is quiet, no cars passing by. Dark storefronts stare back at her, closed for the night. She's in the middle of a barren strip of road, where there's no one who can help her. She'd just needed oat milk for the morning, the bag now swinging heavy at her side. It hadn't seemed like a big deal to walk to the little grocery store while Stephen was out with the car. This was a fairly safe neighborhood. She'd made the walk a million times with no issues.

They hadn't paid her any attention when she'd walked by, at first. Maybe they hadn't noticed her yet. They were loud, the smell of alcohol and cigarettes drifting on the air in a bubble of odor from them. They stood on the pavement of the parking lot, leaning against a large pickup truck. There was a bar in the strip mall; they'd probably come from there.

The phone continues to ring, finally going to voicemail. She waits for the beep, still walking at a fast clip. "Stephen, I need you to come pick me up when you get this. I'm walking home from the grocery store. There are some men. Please hurry."

Rainey ends the call and ponders what to do next. Icy fear pumps through her veins. Her breaths huff out faster than her pace calls for. Her adrenaline has woken the baby, sending him rolling around inside her belly. He lands a solid kick at the height of her stomach. She places the hand with the phone on it to comfort him, or maybe herself. He kicks her hand, but calms after a moment, though she can tell from his small movements that he's still awake.

"Think you're too good for me, you redskin whore? Can't even turn around and answer me?"

His voice is closer now, angrier. She can almost feel the puffs of breath coming from him. The stench of him is suffocating with her pregnancy-heightened sense of smell. She's afraid to turn and look at him, afraid it will spur him forward faster, be the final straw that sets him into motion.

Her street's coming up, but first she has to turn onto a connecting street and walk past a park. She's afraid of that part of the walk. Here, a car might come by. On her street, there will be other houses, people who might hear what's happening and help her. But the park is large and likely empty at this time of night. She should have waited. She could have eaten toast for breakfast instead of cereal. It now feels as if she had a million other choices she could have made.

It strikes her that maybe he'll leave her alone if she turns to show him her belly. That swollen belly had eliminated the male gaze once it grew past a certain point. Men didn't even give up their seats for her the way they'd offered before she was pregnant. They didn't hold doors for her. Her belly had rendered her invisible, and she hadn't minded that anonymity at all except for a bit when her feet hurt or her arms were full. It had taught her a lot about modern society, that was for sure.

She couldn't outrun him. She couldn't overpower him, especially if his friends chose to catch up and help him. These guys rarely went it alone once the action heated up. She'd seen Stephen pay the price of crossing a certain type of drunk white man. Her brothers, too. It was an American pastime in some places. But as a woman she'd avoided violence. So far.

Rainey brings her phone back up and dials 911. She doesn't know what else to do.

"Who you calling now, you uppity piece of trash? I just wanted a little of your time. You could be friendlier, you know."

"911, what's your emergency?"

She keeps her voice low. "I'm being followed by a man. He's acting very aggressive."

"Where are you, ma'am? Do you know the man?"

"I don't know him. He's yelling at me. I'm on First, just up the way from the grocery store."

"Can you return to the store?"

"He's between it and me. And his friends are back there."

"Is there another business you can see that's open?"

"No. It's all dark here, just a bunch of closed businesses. I'm almost to Pine and then there will be houses, but no businesses."

"I'm sending a patrol unit your way. Chances are, when he sees a car he'll turn back right away. Do you want me to stay on the phone with you?"

"Yes, please. I'm scared. How close is the car?"

"I'm not sure, ma'am. It will be a few minutes, at least. You could let him know you're on the phone with the police, that we're on the way. That could be enough to scare him off."

"Okay."

Rainey takes a deep breath and stops, turning to face the man for the first time. He wears a ratty t-shirt with a flannel over it, jeans, and work boots. His hair is short, sticking up in the back in sweaty spikes like he's been running his hands through it. The sight of her pregnant belly elicits no reaction whatsoever, telling her he's known the entire time she's pregnant, yet still pursued her. He stops and stares back at her, a cocky grin on his face.

"You ready for a little fun?" he asks.

"I'm on the phone with the police. They're on their way here. You should leave." She waits for his reaction, phone still held up to her ear, breath held. Through the line comes the sound of typing. Other voices speak in the background. The quiet rasp of the operator's breathing rattles over the mic.

His expression doesn't change at first. Then he turns and waves to his friends, gesturing them to come his way. They climb into the truck and start it. When he turns back, he winks. "I doubt they'll get here in time."

"Ma'am, did he leave?" The voice on the phone makes her jump.

"No. His friends are coming with the truck."

He steps closer to her and tries to grab the phone.

She yanks it back from him and swings the cheap plastic bag with the oat milk in it.

The arc isn't sufficient, the milk pulling at it so it doesn't swing well. He easily deflects it, but now his expression changes, his brow furrowing, grin disappearing. He narrows his eyes and this time grabs the hand holding the phone, squeezing hard.

The operator's voice sounds distantly from the speaker. Rainey can't make out what he's saying.

The bones in her hand grind and crunch, and still she holds on against the pain. She knows losing custody of the phone will be the end of her. The phone is her lifeline, her chance at hope. It's the only thing keeping her from being completely isolated out here with this man and his friends.

Her hand gives out before her will, the phone falling to the ground. When the man bends to pick it up, she swings the milk again, this time doing it just right. It hits him across the head and sends him to the ground.

She drops the milk and runs. The truck isn't in the parking lot anymore. If she can get back to the store, maybe beat him there, she can go inside and wait until Stephen gets her message, comes to get her. Or have the clerk call for a cab.

It feels weird to be running with all that weight hanging off the front of her. She braces her belly with both hands and does her best. Behind her, tires squeal.

She's gotten farther from the store than she'd realized. The warm beacon of its lights, even the flickering one, shine out, the puddle of light so far away. Her lungs, already struggling to inflate fully on a normal day, ache and fight her all the way. The baby, at least, is still, probably lulled to sleep by all the motion.

Feet now pound behind her.

Rainey puts everything she has into a burst of speed.

The footsteps get louder, closer.

Headlights cast her shadow before her. The shadow lurches and shortens as the truck pulls up beside her.

The shriek of metal announces the opening of a door.

She leaves the sidewalk, trying to cut diagonally across the gravel and clumps of grass, to cut down the distance.

The ligaments on either side of her belly strain and ache.

Footsteps pound.

Rainey is almost to the outer reach of the parking lot lights. Just a few more steps. She screams.

One set of footsteps stops.

For a split second, Rainey thinks perhaps the pursuit has stopped. That the scream has scared them away.

Then a missile hits her mid-back, snapping her head back. The impact comes from behind her at an angle. Rainey twists just enough to not bear the brunt of the fall on her stomach. She tries to scream, to fight, but there's pain everywhere at once. Blows rain down on her. She kicks, strikes out, but when the blows hit her stomach, she has to protect it, rolling into the fetal position.

The man on top of her yells, but she can't make out what he's saying. Words bounce from his lips in a guttural onslaught. Pure rage pours from him.

Something harder than hands and feet slams into her head, making a sound like two rocks clacking together. She hears it both inside and outside her head, the exterior sound sharper, more like an eggshell cracking. Inside it's a dull thud.

It hits her several more times until she blacks out.

#

Remembering brings sensation back all at once. It's still dark, but the darkness has a different quality, one that implies the existence of light nearby. She can't smell or taste anything, nor can she hear, but there are too many agonies to focus on.

Underneath it all, Rainey feels something different.

A deep cramping fills her abdomen. It feels as if her entire stomach is a rock, like it's squeezing hard all over at once.

These pains come one after another, picking up speed. There are sharp pains mixed in with the roiling, cramping pain. She remembers her Lamaze training, but when she tries to breathe through it, that's when she realizes she isn't breathing at all.

Rainey exists as nothing but pain.

The urge to push comes. Alone, afraid, she pushes.

As her son slides from her body, the cramping subsides. All the pain disappears.

And then she's floating outside her body, looking down at it. It's beaten and bloody, her head caved in. One eye stares up at her. Her long, dark hair is matted and full of leaves, white fragments, and blood.

Her body lies in some sort of culvert, the limbs twisted where she's been dropped. Between her legs, something moves, twitches.

A baby's cry rises to her ears.

As Rainey watches, a woman walks by. The woman stops, looks around. She moves over to the edge of the culvert and looks down, squinting. Her hand shoots up to her mouth and she's on her phone right away, calling in help.

Rainey hovers as long as she can. When her infant son is picked up by a police officer, swaddled in a jacket he's pulled from his car, she feels a pull she cannot resist. She goes willingly, knowing her baby is safe, the men long gone.

From death, life. Her story goes on.

A note from the author:

In 2016, the NCIC reported 5,712 missing Indigenous women, girls, and two spirits in the United States, with the DOJ only recording 116 of those cases, due to racial misclassification and misgendering. Other disturbing statistics include:

- 1 in 3 Indigenous women will be raped in her lifetime (USDOJ)
- 4 out of 5 Indigenous women will be impacted by violence (CSVANW)
- Homicide is the 3rd leading cause of death for Indigenous women ages 10-24, 5th for ages 25-34 (CDCHP)
- 95% of cases involving Indigenous women aren't reported by the media, and if they are, they get a single mention (UIHI)
- Indigenous women experience violence at a rate 10x higher than the national rate (CDCHP)
- Indigenous women are twice as likely to experience sexual assault than non-Indigenous women, with 96% of those being perpetrated by non-Indigenous men (USDOJ)

90% of violent crimes against Indigenous women are committed by non-Indigenous men, as per the DOJ. These are not tribal issues, but national ones that, without spreading the word, will continue to grow exponentially in this national epidemic. Here's how you can help:

- Boost the signal—share missing persons reports and articles about the murders of Indigenous women
- Donate to projects that support the MMIWG2 (Missing and Murdered Indigenous Women, Girls, & Two Spirits) movement, such as Native Women's Wilderness, Native Hope, National Indigenous Women's Resource Center, Coalition to Stop Violence Against Native Women (csvanw.org), and MMIWUSA.org
- Advocate and vote for legislation that protects and supports Indigenous women
- Continue to learn more about the movement and the epidemic behind it, and help keep others apprised. A good starting place is the Urban Indian Health Institute (UIHI.org) in addition to the organizations mentioned above

Thank you for taking the time to read this information. That, in itself, is the first step to helping save and improve the lives of our Indigenous women, girls, and two spirits, and to end this human rights crisis.

Pat Tompkins is an editor in northern California. Her photos have appeared in Leavings, Sunlight Press, New Southern Fugitives, and other publications.

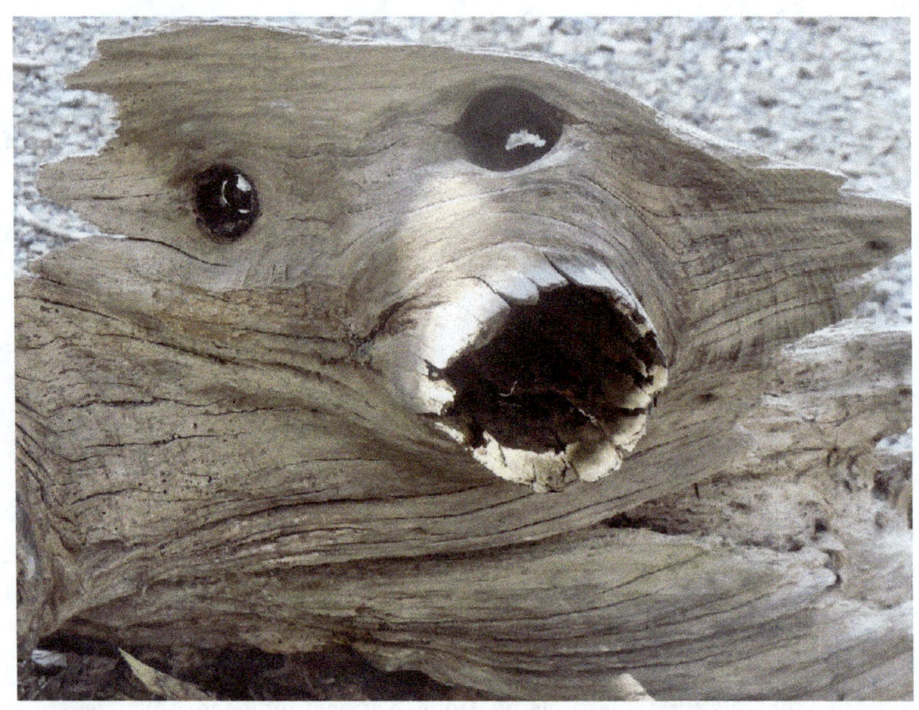

Driftwood Face

I take many photos involving trees but rarely photograph people. Yet I tend to see expressions in trees, anthropomorphizing them. This face reminds me of a dog. Perhaps people should be more like trees. We are only starting to realize how "smart" trees are. I spotted this driftwood in the Mendocino Coast Botanical Gardens in spring 2021.

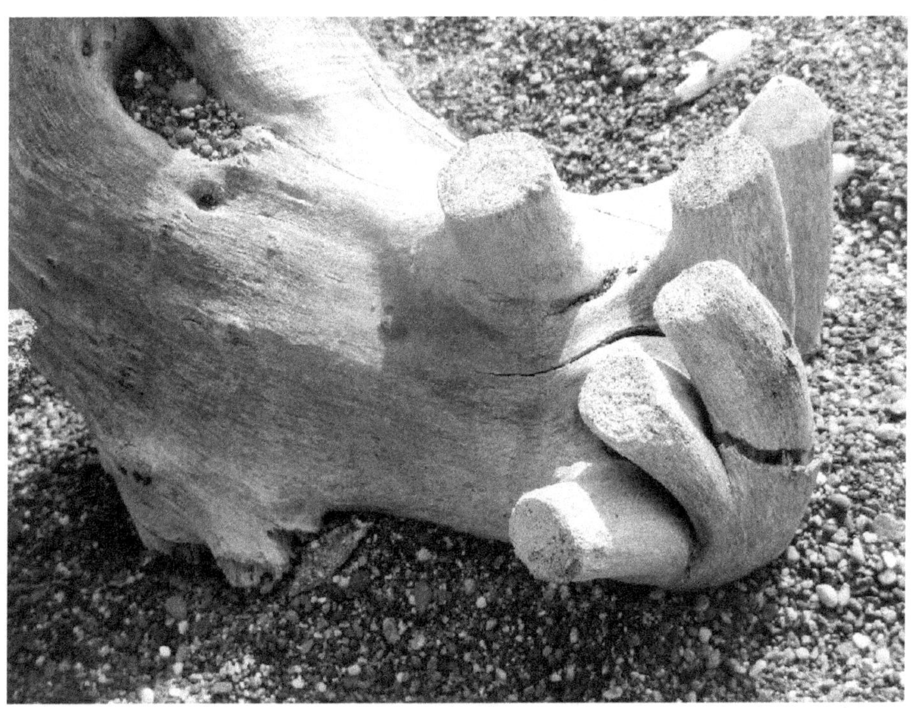

Driftwood Hand

This wooden hand was resting on the beach at Goat Rock Beach near Jenner on the Sonoma County coast. I've long found solace in exploring forests and coastlines, even more since the pandemic has limited my travels.

Asnia Asim's *(she/her) debut chapbook <u>Quarantine with Rilke</u> is forthcoming from Finishing Line Press (2021). Her poetry has received Pushcart nominations from Salamander and Bayou, and Best of the Net from Dialogist. She has published in several print and online journals. She studied poetics at the University of Chicago (2015) where she was awarded an Arts & Humanities Fellowship. Her work has been anthologized in <u>Halal If You Hear Me</u> (Haymarket Books, 2019). She's currently working on her forthcoming novel.*

grandmother's voicemail

Asnia Asim

Heard it's a girl. Your daughter,
do let her be sassy— let her be

like lightning, electric-possessed, brave
in the dark, unlonely, ignoring

the preachers; the sex of her hips
making them afraid, even I

feel a bit terrified for her—
But dear, please teach her

about knives, buy her a ticket
to a place where her worth exceeds

her cute. And keep her body
from becoming another yardstick

for the sins of holy ghosts— let her be
a seeker, of land and air, filled with more,

oh much more, than the evidence
of damage— let the flex of her waist,

her nudity sprawl unbroken,
keeping the world awake. O phenomenal

vamp of the unborn, fertile and chaotic,
badass goddess we look up to, hopeful—

Please let her be.

When the Occupying Troops Withdraw

after Wisława Szymborska's The End and the Beginning

The feast of blood doesn't end.
Someone has to step up.
The capital city won't gnaw
its own heart, after all.

Someone has to claim the tanks
left in the middle of the road,
so the mass graves
have enough bodies to eat.

Someone has to refurbish
the language of victory and beauty,
and declare the dead children victorious,
their empty schools: beautiful.

Someone has to give machine guns
the blessing of his own God.
Someone has to become the voyeur
of terrified girls,
has to be ready to fire a bullet,
just in case.

The eventual silence
is cold and raw.
It will last decades.

World leaders will gather
round another jewel-shaped land,
think of new ways
of packaging shrapnel
for its street-soccer boys,
their bright-colored socks.

While back in the country
they abandoned, wind will whistle
through the blown up piers
and failed state banks.

Power outages will settle
into houses on top of hills.
Eyes will get tired
from looking out for weapons
in the dark.

But some matriarch, hookah in mouth,
still smells like the past.
A newborn's mouth suckles
at some breast that still has milk.
Photos of lost sons
hang crooked on the walls.

Out on the balcony,
sometimes an old man still argues
with himself about the clothes
women shouldn't wear.

On the rooftop that has absorbed
seismic bombs and rainstorms,
someone is making love
to someone, hands clutching hips,
under their bare feet
the dark earth slowly spinning.

*This story is a fragment from the very brief time **Max King Cap** (he/him) spent as a Chicago firefighter. He took the test as a whim when he was an undergraduate. Five years later and a semester from finishing his MFA they called him. He went. Most days he was a visual artist and none of his art friends knew what he really did for a living.*

The Woman in the Sewer
Max King Cap

If the police had been called first, then usually we were only called to the scene for cleanup. Our thick rubber boots, musketeer tall, could be folded to any expedient height. Our fluid resistant coats were easily hosed free of bio matter. That made us indispensable to coppers who were too dainty to soil themselves in the muck of human members and entrails. This run was just for the truck. No engine. No ambulance. Only Truck 66, merely two blocks away, down Coolidge Avenue. A run like this was not unusual. Not in the Loughburgh neighborhood. In Loughburgh, degradations of the body were common. It was early autumn, cloudy and muggy. It was the first run of the day, about eleven thirty on a Saturday morning. I was watching my university, Northwestern, being clobbered by a real football school; Iowa or Nebraska, I don't remember. Then the alarm rang. And we answered, slowly. The incident was grisly but not an emergency. No first aid, no ambulance run. Nothing to be done but removal. There was no pain. There was no blood. Not like I would see that night.

On the corner opposite the firehouse and just a few yards from the "L" tracks was a squat brick tavern named The Silver Dollar. Both its shingle and façade displayed a black and gray rendering of an obverse Liberty coin, crudely painted and badly faded, radiate head left. Native Americans, coerced by the Indian Relocation Act, and Appalachians, cast aside by mining concerns, both arrived in the Loughburgh neighborhood during the same decade to find far more poverty than liberty. Suspicious of their new surroundings yet needful to socialize, many of them discovered, then frequented, then haunted The Silver Dollar, and it is there that their blood regularly flowed. The opposite of The Silver Dollar was just few blocks east, an elegant and storied jazz club called The Green Mill. Its patrons dressed sharply and ordered vintage cocktails. The satirical proximity was never lost on me when I sat in a booth at The Green Mill, only a slightly less brief distance from my firehouse yet a place where there was no danger of encountering my colleagues. They all lived miles away on the Northwest Side, in an all-White private ghetto reserved for cops and firemen, and they considered Loughburgh, despite its wealth of listed architecture, an unredeemable shantytown.

The human brain is a glutton for blood, the eyes and the facial muscles are similarly thirsty. Consequently, injuries to the head, even minor ones, bleed ostentatiously. In an unfortunate parallel, the human mind is a voracious collector, and its most accumulative archive is labeled *insult*. These biological and psychological truths collided every weekend night, just thirty feet from our firehouse. But on these nights our ambulance was invariably absent; it was obliged to attend to more serious calamities. That left us, the hose-haulers and axe-carriers, to perform first aid, something that was only cursorily covered during what I remember as a single day at the fire academy.

The Silver Dollar had a two a.m. license. At two thirty a.m. many of its customers were still in front of the tavern. Unable to continue drinking but uneager to return home they gathered on the sidewalk, under the sepia tint of the sodium vapor streetlamp, imagining perhaps that if they waited long enough the bar might change its mind and reopen, like a stage performer coaxed into an encore. There never was, but still they would linger, growing nostalgic already for drinks and frolic that had been curtailed. So, they became frustrated. There was a routine. An insult would be inferred. An argument would start. Then someone would step in to break it up and immediately someone else would attempt to halt that effort. I knew what was happening. I could hear it. But I had to prepare for what inevitably happened next.

The patrons' worn and faded T-shirts—Phil Collins: Both Sides of the World, Bulls NBA Champs 3-Peat—were likely purchased from the nearby Am-Vets thrift store, but when their wearers shuffled toward the firehouse for post-fight repair their t-shirts were far from faded; they were vivid with fresh blood.

The loser of the fight always presented himself alone—required presumably by custom to surrender his crew like captured chess pieces—and I recollected my training doubtfully and invented treatment on the spot. I was on third watch, midnight to eight. Someone was always awake in the glazed brick cubicle near the front door of the firehouse. It was to this human-sized door that people in need could walk up and ask for help, a small gray door that appeared a mere afterthought compared to the three enormous red doors that reared up noisily and spat out the truck, the engine, and the ambulance; hastily screaming toward the locality of dire and less elective trauma.

The candidate was always on third watch so the senior firefighters could sleep. The Silver Dollar bleeders came to me. That night I entertained three. Three unwise men. That night was the same day of the body in the manhole. One might think such an image would be seared indelibly into my memory, but I hadn't thought about her—I had witnessed so many other degradations of the human body that she soon ceased to stand out—until a few years later when I recalled watching the NBA Finals on my local tavern television.

#

The Torchlight wasn't fancy, just a neighborhood hangout where Lincoln crosses Roscoe, but compared to The Silver Dollar it seemed like the Oak Bar at the Plaza. On slow Sunday afternoons one could listen to a strange skinny fellow sing acapella jazz, years before he became a famous bandleader. It was also, mercifully, not a sports bar. I can't stand sports bars; the noise, the contrived bonhomie, the multiple flashing television screens that transform the sporting event into an eye-wearying clutter. Sports bars denature the game, making it subservient to the total- immersion-oversized beer-buffalo-wing-industrial complex. They are the opposite of relaxation. In my local tavern, three blocks from my apartment and only one-third full, game five was playing on a normal-sized television until the Knicks and the Rockets were interrupted by breaking news: a former football star and rental car pitchman was leading police on a low-speed chase along some California freeway. On the court Hakeem Olajuwon had just been called for a three-second violation and was complaining to the ref, as athletes seem to do by reflex, that he was completely innocent. He gave the traditional silent performance, his face a Grecian mask of tragedy, that clearly protested, "How could I, a seasoned professional, be guilty of such a silly violation, something that even junior high students are too savvy to commit?"

We didn't see the referee's reaction because of the cutaway to the White Bronco. Immediately an insulted howl arose in the tavern. I didn't howl —the Rockets eventually triumphed over the Knicks, four games to three (I hated the Knicks; John Starks was an evil little prick)—I was having a flashback of another scene in another bar, a déjà vu of another news event that commandeered a sporting event. A little girl, a baby really, Jessica McClure, was being rescued from a well where she had been trapped for two days. I had watched the rescue of Baby Jessica at a bar in the gallery district, Club Lago, on another mercifully small television. Club Lago is a Chicago staple, a half-century old red brick shotgun with a chamfered doorway at the corner of Superior and Orleans streets. The River North gallery district—born out of abandoned printing companies that fled to the suburbs for horizontal ease—was now half its former size. Many galleries scattered in the wake of the giant warehouse fire that consumed, in one vast hot breath, dozens of high ceilings, heavy beams, and works of art. Though the artists substantially fled south and west as River North became prohibitively pricey, Club Lago remained a rendezvous for kitschy nostalgia.

The rescue of Baby Jessica interrupted the seventh game of the National League Championship (Cardinals prevailed over Giants four games to three) but I made no protest. I was having a drink with another artist, a former professor, mentor, and friend, Corado. An abstract painter who misspent his youth in second-run cinemas, he liked meeting at Club Lago because it reminded him of the Pentangeli strangling scene in *Godfather Part II*. He outlined to me the similarity of the media circus surrounding Baby Jessica to the film of a similar name, *The Big Circus*, now better known by its original title, *Ace in the Hole*. In that film a man is trapped in a cave collapse and self-serving reporter Kirk Douglas takes deadly advantage of the man's predicament. It was a cynical view of sensational journalism and the monetization of tragedy. It conveyed me back to another vulgar transaction, the coppers who gave us a fifth of cheap whiskey to do their dirty work, to extract the woman from the sewer, lift her out of the manhole with the roof ladder, seal her in the black rubber body bag, then place her in the back of a paddy wagon. I told the story to Corado. He alone was privy to my secret past as a city worker (I kept it a secret so long some of my art friends do not believe me). He is the only one to whom I have told this particular story. Except now. Now, I'm telling it to you.

#

The first man came in sheepishly; the fight must have not only sobered but humbled him. He was tall and wide but soft, as if he never considered exercise. His belly peaked out from below his t-shirt which bore a narrowing red stripe pointing up to his left eye. I was not startled by the blood —I was surprisingly impervious to bodily degradations. Perhaps that makes me thoughtless or insensitive; I had seen senior firefighters wince and turn away or vomit (one lieutenant nearly fainted) when we were presented with a bodily vandalization, but not me, I never did. I was more concerned by the possibility that I would exhaust all my gauze and antiseptic that night and would require assistance, that I would be thought incompetent—at a firehouse where I was already unwelcome. I knew more were coming, judging from the noise I had heard outside The Silver Dollar, and since the ambulance was gone supplies might not last.

I asked him his name and he mumbled Enoch, or something like that, and I examined his eye, the lid dyed with his blood. He was a tall, doughy Native American. He smelled of beer from both this night and last night. I cleaned the surrounding area as tenderly as I could and was delighted to find that it was a very small cut on the upper orbit of his eye, the ridge at the top of the left eye socket. I protected his eye with gauze while I cleaned the wound, drying then sealing it with a pair of butterflies. He didn't wince or even speak during the procedure. He said nothing but *Enoch* when he arrived and *thank you* when he departed. He had been punched or struck or had fallen but it was nothing serious. He was a very lucky man. He was going home, or something very like it. At least he was alive. It had been a good day for Enoch.

#

A manhole cover is exceptionally heavy, well over two hundred pounds, bone-breakingly heavy and deadly. In nineteen thirty-seven, in

Chicago's Logan Square neighborhood, an underground explosion launched several manhole covers high into the air. One of them crashed through the skylight atop a five-story building and hurtled down the elevator shaft, killing the operator and injuring two others. There are also many designs. Choose your big city, it is likely that a set of drink coasters impressed with manhole cover designs can be easily found. There is even an artist in Germany who uses them like printing presses, inking their elaborate surfaces then laying pristine t-shirts or tote-bags over them and transferring the imprint of the manhole cover; she applies the pressure with an outsized rubber rolling pin. Often stolen when metal prices spike, some covers are works of fine and collectible industrial art. Some are sewer covers, others for electrical cable. The electrical covers are solid, but the sewer covers are perforated in a spider web pattern to allow the heavy rain and melting snow to vacate the street. Had it been a solid cover the woman might not have been discovered for months, perhaps a year.

Lifting a manhole cover requires either incredible strength and a good friend similarly endowed (the hard way) or a purpose-designed tool (the easy way). Although there are several tools made by competing companies specifically for this task, we carried on our truck a multiple use tool called a halligan, named after a clever firefighter from the days of yore. I knew exactly where the halligan was kept because every morning I had to account for all the tools on the truck. I would go to the captain's bunkroom—the captain and the lieutenant had private bunkrooms—for the clipboard with the checklist, then back to the truck where I would test the roof saw, two pulls usually got it started, and account for every tool on the list. There was always one tool missing. It hadn't been part of the standard equipment for years, but the checklist had been endlessly reprinted and distributed and no one had bothered to update the document, nor did I ever suggest it.

#

First aid claimant number two had a hill folk accent and was incredibly pale. He had thinning red hair and could not have weighed more than a hundred and forty pounds. His nose was bleeding in three ways, both nostrils and a small cut on the bridge. Fresh blood still flowed over the drying blood on his lips and chin and dripping from the end of his nose. He, like many of The Silver Dollar crowd, was a dedicated drinker, and as alcohol consumption interferes with hemostasis—I did learn something down at the fire academy after all—his bleeding continued. His problem could be compared to a charged fire hose. Essentially, when a fire hose is connected to a hydrant, one can turn off the water at the hydrant (decrease the flow from the blood vessel) or at the nozzle at the end of the hose (stanch by blood coagulation). His body was unable to employ either of these strategies. I did not learn this man's name because he did not seem to understand my questions and spoke only in random run-on sentences. I held my finger in front of my mouth like a primary school teacher so he would stop talking; that worked only briefly. I needed to clean off some of the blood in order for the tape to stick. He could only be aided by a massive pillow of gauze taped to the bridge of his nose, and a pair of rolled gauze logs shoved up his nostrils. He winced momentarily at the procedure. "OK, you're done," I said. He then nodded and waved his hand over his shoulder as he went back into the street. I watched him from the door as he walked unsteadily toward a gathering of men on the corner. I waved the next gentlemen into the office.

#

When we arrived the cops pointed us toward the manhole. It was behind a building we had visited before, for another dead woman, who had been near the top of the formerly elegant Art Deco high-rise that cast a shadow on the manhole. It was humid and our heavy coats and boots made walking even a few yards somewhat steamy. A last-of-the-season ice cream truck was somewhere nearby, I could hear its jingly rendition of Stephen Foster's *Camptown Races.* When we looked down through the sewer grate we saw the woman. So might have anyone who passed by. The manhole was in a driveway not twenty feet from a busy shopping sidewalk. But who looks down into the sewer? One person, at least, did. They called the cops. The cops called us.

The driveway opened onto a large parking lot that was ringed with apartment buildings, many with back porches, and the rear entrances of the shops that fronted that same busy shopping sidewalk. The cops redirected pedestrians. Some were no doubt perturbed to have to walk all the way around the block to reach their cars by an alternate entrance, but we couldn't have civilians seeing what we were about to do. This was murder. Obviously, murder. She certainly didn't commit suicide by wrapping herself in plastic, crawling into the sewer, then dragging the two hundred and fifty pound grate over her.

She was nearly enveloped in two heavy-duty trash bags, secured by silver duct tape. Her bottom half was submerged. Her top half was mostly submerged. Her body was bent over arcing toward us and the bags had separated to expose her right side just above her waist. That is why we presumed it was a woman, a waist-high flounce of a black skirt could be seen just barely above water level. Several of her ribs, the actual bones, were visible through a large wound that did not appear to have been caused by human violence. Rats, I suspected, because the sinew between the ribs was irregularly but methodically removed; sawtooth ridges of tendon edged the spaces between. McGee and I walked back to the truck to remove the gear we needed for this unusual job. It would be pure improvisation because this scenario was not covered at the fire academy. McGee chose the items: the halligan, and a roof ladder. I carried the ladder. A halligan is a three-headed tool capable of extreme violence, mostly for striking, puncturing, and prying.

At one end of the heavy rod is a flattened claw, and at the other a narrow axe set perpendicular to a ferocious pick. A roof ladder is an aluminum straight ladder equipped with fold-away hooks at one end. Its chief purpose is to grab the peak of a pitched roof in order to give a firefighter purchase on the steep incline and create a makeshift stairway. But we did not employ these tools for those purposes. We had also brought a body bag.

There is a notch on the edge of a manhole cover, placed rather like the sipping hole on the top of an open soda can. McGee slipped the adze end of the halligan into this notch, rocked it slightly backward, dislodging the cover, then flipping the halligan over to crook and drag the iron disc smoothly, if quite noisily, away from the manhole. It was a deft maneuver, and I was jealous of the ease with which he did it. This is how the outrageous weight of the iron cover is defeated, not by lifting but by dragging. Now that the cover was off we could see her more clearly. It was such a degrading act, I thought. Then more questions came into my mind. I did that. It annoyed my colleagues. "God, you're worse than my grandson, with your questions, and he's only seven years old," Holman, our frustrated engineer, said when I asked about how exactly the fire engine works (essentially, it is a step-up transformer).

How does one coordinate the placing of a body in a sewer? Was she dead when she went in? How many people conspired to plant her there? Without the proper tools it requires a good deal of work to remove a manhole cover, particularly to do it quietly, and alone. How do you convince someone to help you dispose of a body? Someone had to see it. Hear it. Why didn't they call? All those back porches and no witnesses? What had happened before she was placed there? Was it a friendly get-together, with alcohol, with drugs, until something went wrong? Did it begin simply as a lovers' quarrel? Could it have been the rage of a violent and jealous husband? Or was it planned? Did she have a cat waiting at home, moaning loudly for food, water, and her warm lap? Did she have a loud, honking laugh? I couldn't unpuzzle these circumstances and none of these questions did I ask out loud because McGee was even less generous than Holman. He did not think beyond the job at hand and when the work was done he preferred paperback mysteries.

#

The third man entered then stopped, looking me up and down. He seemed surprised that a Black firefighter was now at the formerly all-White firehouse. Surprised and displeased. He was missing a tooth. I had no idea what he expected me to do about that. He seemed to know this and did not ask. I was relieved to see that the back of his head was cut. I could attend to that wound. In his high and raspy voice, he ordered me to hurry up. He was one of those sinewy, prickly troublemakers to whom everything is a personal insult. His muscles were taut, and his attitude was mouthy. His arms were scraped and there was dirt and bits of glass in the tiny wounds. Someone had really mopped the street with him. "That hurts—!" He stopped short and glared at me and I could tell he was about to call me a name that would have gotten him punched in the mouth. He thought better of it. He quieted down. His hair was dyed a cheap and artificial brown while his chin showed gray stubble and his accent said Tennessee. He reminded me of the one-armed boy I knew briefly. He had lost the arm, before he arrived at my military school, while trying to hop a train. The loss haunted him and guided his behavior. He wasn't precisely trying to show us how tough he was, but clearly determined to prove that even though he had just one arm, he wasn't weak, to prove himself to himself. But he had become addicted to the loss that could never be restored, so he rejected his prosthesis, as if eager to be forever punished for that foolish bit of railroad bravado, spurred by that mysterious chemical that intoxicates boyhood and stays in the bloodstream forever. He was handsome in a beachboy fashion, blonde, blue-eyed, and slim, but he wasted no time in attempting to exorcise what he perceived as a deficiency. It was as if his phantom limb was a living, cantankerous cudgel, ever driving him cholerically forward. He sneered at camaraderie, he insulted everyone he met, he started fights over innocent glances or laughter heard from a distance. This bizarre conduct not only predictably failed but backfired into numerous unprovoked fistfights—and he didn't stand a chance with one arm. Eventually, I too had to beat him up. I felt bad. Poor kid. Halfway through the semester he was gone.

The southerner remained silent as I plucked glass from his arms but winced at the antiseptic. It was a lengthy process. I imagined someone dragging him through an alley. I patched the back of his head and sent him on his way. As he was nearly out the door he turned and spat out, "Thanks for nothing."

It didn't anger me. These men were hapless, lucky drunks. Their elective trauma was negligible compared to what I had seen that morning. These men could not know the terror, the violence, that this woman endured; could not imagine that moment when she realized that this would be the end of her life, that she would never see anyone, ever, again.

#

McGee and I stood on either side of the manhole, the police now watching us instead of restraining the onlookers, and lowered the roof ladder by its rails, hooks splayed, gloves on, and hand over hand, matching each other's movements until we could submerge the ladder deeply enough to gently gaff the woman's underside and begin to slowly lift out her body. We had to go lower than we expected because of her contortion and clasped the ladder by the last couple of rungs to make sure we would not lose our grip. Once we were finally confident that we had secured a purchase on her body we reversed our motions, hand under hand, to raise her. The black trash bags sagged with the weight of the water and exposed more of her debased body.

The bag that covered her head slipped, returning its water to the black stream below, then fell off completely and we could see more readily the degradation of the remains; from the lower side of her head long, dark hair rained putrid water as we lifted her slumped body upward. As soon as she rose above water level a reeking wave of putrefaction clouded around us, a fume of sewer water and decomposition. It then drifted toward the policemen and the onlookers, and they erupted in a collective gasp. We kept lifting, hand under hand, and since her slender body was unevenly ballasted, we were especially careful not to damage her corpse any more grievously by roughly striking her against the side of the manhole. Her head had been completely submerged for so long— for how long we did not know—that her face changed as we raised her; it was a malleable mass. It was pale and doughy and the features were distorted but the most macabre aspect was that even in death she moved; her hidden, submerged face had been set in motion, transforming as we watched her rise. Her face appeared to detach at the hairline and her skin slid down her skull, buckling like a faulty theatre curtain, until it rutched at what would have been the level of her eyebrows, compacting her entire face into a stack of slick, fatty ripples.

Our black, rubber body bag was already unzipped—the police had resumed their duties of shooing away onlookers—and we lifted and contorted her dripping body into it. The smell was biting to the nostrils, eye-watering, and she resisted enclosure because of her ragdoll floppiness. Once zippered in we carried her to the police van. McGee returned to the sewer and loudly replaced the manhole cover. I secured the roof ladder to the side of the truck. There would be a thorough hosing-down required when we returned to the firehouse. As I was packing up and McGee was talking to a police sergeant— it appeared they knew each other, probably from their segregated neighborhood—another officer tapped me delicately on the shoulder. Fearful of muck he was wearing rubber gloves. When I turned around, he said, "Thanks," and held out a small paper bag. I took the bag and looked inside. It was a fifth of whiskey, its overly ornate label and deceptively regal name marked it as a cheap and careless gesture. I remember it as being named Lord Gregory, or Earl of Stirlingshire, or some similarly concocted nonsense. The liquor store was just across the street; it had a garish yellow façade and its biggest offering was lottery tickets.

That was all she was going to get, though. An afterthought communion celebrated with sips of the Earl of Stirlingshire (none for me, thanks), raised from a watery tomb and placed in a sepulcher that was a stainless-steel cubicle on wheels; she was the event, but only briefly. Those who were watching from their porches had gone back inside. The shoppers resumed checking off the items from their lists. We drove back to the firehouse, passing by The Green Mill.

After an overly hot shower I went back to the tv room. The game was over, the television was off. I stared at the blank screen and replayed the event in my head. I concocted a story of comeuppance for those who had gotten away with murder, like something from one of McGee's paperbacks, and wondered, if this was the morning, what would the night hold for me.

KC Grifant *(she/her) is a New England-to-SoCal transplant who writes internationally published horror, fantasy, science fiction and weird western stories for collectible card games, podcasts, anthologies and magazines. Her writings have appeared in Andromeda Spaceways Magazine, Unnerving Magazine, Colp, Tales to Terrify and others. Her short stories have haunted dozens of collections, including <u>We Shall Be Monsters</u>; <u>Shadowy Natures: Tales of Psychological Horror</u>; <u>The One That Got Away-Women of Horror Anthology</u>; <u>Beyond the Infinite: Tales from the Outer Reaches</u>; <u>Six Guns Straight From Hell Volume 3</u>; and the Stoker-nominated <u>Fright Mare: Women Write Horror</u>. For details, visit www.KCGrifant.com or amazon.com/author/kcgrifant.*

The Circus King
KC Grifant

1

The Circus King slid into her customary grin as the first guests shuffled into the tent. She lifted the scepter that lay next to her—occasionally it took the form of a whip, or a long staff—and greeted families from atop her perch.

"Gather gals and ghouls! Feast on fantastic feats of fascination . . . astounding aerial acrobatics . . . dazzling and delightful dancers . . . clever and capricious clowns!" The Circus King said, her voice rich in a decades-old smoker's baritone. The Circus King's words fell with little effort. Sometimes she tried to form other words. "*Where am I,*" or "*help,*" but only shrill declarations of the show would manifest.

Peanut shells and popcorn kernels crunched under the guests' feet, like so many casings of a swarm of insects that had hatched all at once.

The Circus didn't sell peanuts.

It didn't sell anything.

And yet, the tickets and the peanuts and the candy and cups of soda all appeared.

A single yellow light fell on the Circus King, a perfect concentric outline on her perch next to the stage. A little girl with a blue candy-stained mouth gaped up at her, until the Circus King widened her smile, so large until it seemed she would swallow up the whole tent. For this performance, Circus King took the shape of a round man with a shelf-like nose, a moustache worthy of a twirl, and tufts of orange hair. Her crown had taken the form of a towering hat.

"Delight in devilish dances! Leer at lunging leapers . . . juggling jesters . . . mega merrymakers! Indulge in ingénues incredible!"

A wisp of nighttime air, warm and salty, swirled in with the visitors from the open flap in the tent. The Circus King sometimes tried to look out through the entrance from her perch but her thoughts would grow murky. The Circus's way of saying *no*. Whether it was the tenth or hundredth performance, the Circus King couldn't remember. Time blurred in the tent, smudged beneath the shadows of the guests.

"Ready, rousing rascals? Revel, relish and reel . . . see sights so staggering . . . frolic in the festivity of fools and fiends!"

As soon as the last person sat in the last seat, the show began. Clowns flew out from their hiding spots, too small or too large or too round to be real humans. The audience cheered as one beat another with an oversized mallet, other clowns egging on the violence. Pink and blue blood splattered out of the beaten clown, who grabbed its rainbow entrails and screeched.

Another performer, large as an ape and with a crimson face, knocked over the group.

The audience laughed harder.

The Circus hummed, pleased.

The Circus King didn't know much, only that the Circus wanted this. The more she could coax the audience to give into their frenetic energy, the better the creatures performed.

The show continued, with acrobats flicking across the ring like larger-than-life crickets. The Circus King imagined stunts and the performers executed them, as if someone had scraped out a window to her mind and all the creatures could catch a glimpse. Though the costumes and colors changed, her show stayed the same.

Except for tonight.

A new, green-tinged creature wove between the jugglers tossing sticks of fire. The trickster bumped into one of the jugglers' knees and fell over.

Some of the audience laughed, thinking it was a routine. But it wasn't routine; it was a wrinkle in her otherwise flawless show.

The Circus King refocused past her irritation and continued to shout.

"Prepare for perplexing possibilities! The fantastic fiery finale! Dazzling, delirious and death-defying!"

The green trickster leapt and gestured, trying to get the viewers' attention, but all of their eyes fixed on the grand finale: dancers leaping through rainbow-colored rings of fire that descended from the ceiling. The Circus King reveled in their applause, in the Circus's approval.

Once the last of the audience had left, the music and light dissipated and the tent shrunk and sealed itself shut. Usually after a performance, the creatures climbed and clung to one another in a pile of flesh, some fornicating in the shadows. The Circus King would doze above on her perch, limbs heavy, as they all waited in a drowsy twilight. When the time came to perform again, the Circus would alert her, the lights would come back on.

But this time, something was amiss.

"Hyucka Hyucka Hyucka!" Some of the clowns made the facsimile of a laugh during the performance, and continued it now as they ran in a circle along with other creatures, unseeing eyes bright as plastic.

The Circus King leapt down from her perch and snapped her scepter against the ground. The creatures ignored it. She moved them aside, their bulbous flesh yielding to her scepter. They circled a blot marring the ground.

"What is this?" the Circus King murmured.

A hole, about the size of a fist. The floor of the Circus varied—this time it appeared as cracked wood, strewn with hay and peanuts and the droppings of some animal.

She circled the hole. Her crown throbbed at her head, heavy enough to snap her neck in two.

The creatures paused. Not quite turned toward her and not quite toward the hole either. One of the clown's mouths looked like a gnash that needed sewing. The Circus King didn't know what any of them were made of, only that she had once seen this clown bend over, its button strained and popped to reveal nothing but darkness beneath the streaked polka dots. Next to it, the new greenish trickster, tinier than the rest, watched her intently.

She turned back to studying the hole. No draft came from it, only a peculiar smell that she couldn't quite place but made her uneasy, that lifted a small crack in the back of her mind, a bend at the baseboard of the few thoughts she could manage.

Another one of the Circus's many tricks. The Circus King couldn't bring herself to get closer to peer down the hole. They were in the Circus's belly and whatever sat at its core lay in that darkness. Something about it felt ravenous, boding.

Maybe tomorrow it would go away.

2

As the Circus King dozed and waited for the next show, snatches of memories came back to her, unleashed from their cage, as if the hole in the ground had prompted an opening in her mind.

She remembered pigtails against her ears and sugar-crusted lips. She had been with her father. *Pa.* A great longing swept her, past the feeling of a cotton candy stick, wisps curling against her sticky fingers. The sun sinking low behind them had cast ribbons of shadow and light on the water beyond the pier. Pa's grimy nails pressed into a black-and-white flyer.

"It'll be fun."

Evelyn, that was her name, it came to her now and again—Evelyn remembered the dread she had felt when she and her father turned away from the boardwalk, away from the crowds, and down an alleyway in the tiny coastal town. They and a few others headed toward the circus, set far back from the pier.

"It'll be fun," Pa kept saying. "Maybe we'll see the world's smallest man or acrobats."

The tent loomed in great red and white stripes, shining with newness. The first few drops of rain flicked off its surface as though the Circus lived under its own force field. It whispered, its stripes shuddering in the wind.

Evelyn had stopped. She didn't want to go into the tent. She dropped the cup of soda. Her dress was a mess. Pa's brow darkened, telling her to be more careful. It was her nice dress, ruined. She didn't care, didn't even like the dress. He gave her a warning slap on the arm, the jolt sending her cotton candy flying to the ground. She watched in horror as the delicate pink candy darkened next to her shoes.

She cried, but Pa chided her again before turning on his heel and marching toward the tent, leaving her to follow.

The tent ahead of her flapped as if to get her attention but she looked down at her ruined treat, raindrops catching in her lashes as she wished with all her might that she would never see Pa again. Wisps of the cotton candy against the damp bricks morphed, spreading into wings. Hardened nubs of the candy lengthened like a spine, as fluffs of pink expanded and enveloped her.

Evelyn had emerged, stretching and straining in the Circus's spotlight on her perch, speaking her ringmaster lines as if in a dream. It was where she had been ever since.

Evelyn shuddered the inchoate mass of sensation and memory away, her fingers—far too long—flapping like banners against her moist cheeks. The crown, like wrought iron, seared into her scalp.

She was the Circus King now.

Nevertheless she remembered. Her plastic shoes full of pebbles. Strands of cotton candy hardening into pink commas against the bricks in the rain. Her palms, streaked and empty.

3

The next night, the hole had grown five feet at least. The creatures performed dutifully around it but the Circus King had other problems. The unwelcome trickster had returned, ruining her show.

"See succulent and surreal sights!" The Circus King shouted to the rapt audience. "Sassy simpletons soaring sublimely!"

The green trickster marched up to the audience between the sword-swallowing act and the contortionist. The trickster stuck one foot in the air and jumped up like a cannonball, leaving a trail of green and blue feathers in its wake.

"Disbelieve daring deeds!" The Circus King continued. "Prepare your popping peepers . . ."

The trickster continued to pop up and down, spinning in the air and shedding feathers like a sick bird as visitors clapped and strained to grab the feathers. A completely new performance that the Circus King had no control over.

". . . for the fantastical fiery finale!"

For this performance, the Circus had transformed Evelyn into someone with more girth than she was used to. Her belly swelled under satin fabric and she wore a hat that seemed to reach halfway up to the tent. She barked the laugh of an old man about to reveal a wicked secret.

The end couldn't come fast enough. After the crowd left, the Circus King leapt down, using her prop—now a jewel-studded staff—to push the performers aside. Half a dozen dancers shimmered in their outfits like nighttime beetles. The clowns with their painted grins turned toward her, grimly attentive. She resisted stepping back. She would not retreat; she was the Circus King.

"What do you want?" she said to the hole, and the creatures.

As usual, the clowns didn't react, aside from the occasional "hyucka." Their eyes bore into her, white and matte, no more effective than pasted squares of paper. They watched with something else, smell or sound or another sense the Circus King was unaware of.

The hole gaped in the center as Evelyn neared its edge. Its inkiness suggested an unthinkable depth, stretching to the other side of the planet and beyond. A hint of something else wafted in that vastness, something not of this world. It was the same presence that had grown the Circus and its performers in a monstrous shell, with Evelyn at its center like a pearl.

Everything in Evelyn told her to run from that hole. She thought of her pa, the ocean breeze, and marched to the edge of the tent to stab the fabric with her staff. No way through. She swung around, and brought her staff against the nearest clown who soared a few feet as if it were made of pillows stitched together. It landed with a giggle and neon blue splatter.

"I'll smash them all," Evelyn said between breaths. "If you don't let me out."

The trickster emerged from the group. Unlike the others, its eyes were cold, calculating. Seeing.

It gestured to itself emphatically, as if to say *mine*. Though the creature was small, with bulging cheeks and hair like yarn, some human features remained. It glared at her with eyes all too human, resentful and full of rage.

It gestured again. *Mine.*

"You wished too. To be here," The Circus King said and her baritone had vanished, a higher squeak of a voice returning. *Evelyn's* voice. "Well it was a mistake. A trick. You can have this horrible circus. I'll leave."

Evelyn jumped when she saw her hands—still far too long but thinner, smoother, than she had seen in a long time. Her own oval nails hovered beneath the shadows that streamed over her skin. The tight band around her temples flared. She tried to yank off the crown, but it felt embedded on her head.

One of the performers spoke. A smaller clown, with a painted orange smile. "Hyucka. Only one." Its words were thick and squished like mud splatters. It sounded like a pile of worms that had joined together to try to mimic human speech.

"One," the clown managed again. It lifted its white hands, bulky like stitched stubs of fungi-covered sausages. It pointed to the hole. "Waste."

Evelyn understood now. The trickster contended for her crown, to be a new Circus King who could offer fresh visions. But that would mean Evelyn would have to be disposed of.

The trickster neared her, less the size of a child and more Evelyn's own height now. She couldn't tell if she was shrinking or it was growing.

"Whatever happened to you, the Circus doesn't make it better," Evelyn said. "But have it. Here." She tried again to wretch off the crown but it held steady, branded into her skin. "Let me leave!"

But there was no way out, all openings were sealed aside from the terrible pit. She'd rather be Circus King forever than face that unnatural darkness. The pit wasn't freedom. It was worse than death, that much was clear, clear as the growing impatience that emanated from it. She would be cast out, far from this Earth, into the bowels of some region from which she could never return.

Evelyn tried not to shriek as the performers stepped closer, locking her and the trickster around the hole. It was simple to them. One Circus King stayed, one Circus King left.

The Circus breathed, waiting.

The trickster, the child, whatever it was, had crept too close, its sharp hands closing on Evelyn's wrists as it tried to yank her into the hole. Evelyn raised her staff but it deflated like a half-filled balloon. She dropped the staff and kicked the trickster square in its belly. It squealed but held on.

The performers around them shifted, giving them space while they struggled. The pit seemed darker, eager to be filled, to flush out its waste.

Evelyn's ringmaster boots scraping closer to the hole.

"No," she cried and the trickster's white teeth glinted.

Evelyn remembered the heavy reassurance of her pa's hand, wisps of candy dissolving on her tongue mixed in with the scent of ocean air after sunset.

There could only be one Circus King. But there *had* to be one.

Evelyn gritted her teeth and changed her grip to take hold of the trickster's arms. It realized too late what she planned as Evelyn propelled both of them forward.

There *had* to be one.

They plummeted down the hole. The trickster shrieked as Evelyn kicked in the darkness. Her hair grew thin and long and short, her body stretched and shrank and collapsed and expanded.

The sensation of falling stopped. Evelyn floated in the emptiness, the trickster's panicked breathing behind her.

"I'll bring them all down here. Every single one of your contenders," Evelyn said, her words immediately swallowed by the pit. "So you will never have a Circus King."

A pressure bore into her skin on all sides and the crown prickled around her head. She touched her forehead, freed and scrapped raw by the clamp. The darkness flickered like curtains separating, yielding to a softer blackness and her face opened, spreading like the unfolding of a cape.

The trickster floated in front of her, the metal ring clamping around its greenish skin. It grinned at her before it grew, stretching into the Circus King.

Both of them were expelled out in a great rush of wind.

4

Evelyn stood outside, her mind as empty as the icy, ink-stained sky above. She ran her tongue over crushed sugar cubes and burnt kernels, looking for Pa on the boardwalk.

Something was wrong—her clothes didn't fit right, and her hair seemed like someone else's, brushing past her shoulders and out of their pigtails. Her feet ached, too big for her shoes. She had grown taller it seemed, as though she had missed a birthday or two.

Circus music started up nearby, sending a bolt of panic through Evelyn's muddied thoughts. Though her heart hammered and every inch of her told her to run, it seemed important—very important—that she walk slowly, away from the droning music and toward the water, where the moonlight on the waves flickered like a warning. She didn't want to draw the attention of what felt like a massive creature lying just out of reach, resting.

Maybe someone could help her find Pa.

Behind her, the Circus played on.

Derek N. Otsuji *lives and writes on the southern shore of Oahu. He is the author of* <u>The Kitchen of Small Hours</u>, *SIU Press 2021. Recent poems have appeared in The Southern Review, Rattle, Pleiades, Beloit Poetry Journal and The Threepenny Review.*

Grandma's Slims
Derek N. Otsuji

Of necessity, she had made a virtue
of it—the delicious secret vice,
cool mentholated kiss, stolen when we
were out of sight.

Somehow she'd kept it
from us for the whole of her life,
the part I knew, until I went in search

of her, in the garden,
where instead of pulling weeds
in the onion patch, she stood by the hedge

of red hibiscus, blued in isolation,
abstracted, far from chores, bodies needing
to be fed, in an attitude of someone stepping off

into the air—toxic, rarefied—
a precarious freedom—as the live ember
blistered into ash.

And then she saw me,
a child of nine, standing there—silent,
marveling—and she snapped back

to the reality of weeds
and the onions. It was too late
to pretend I didn't see the burning wand

fall to the ground, where she snuffed it
with a twist of her slippered,
slickly polished toe.

Announcing Our Contest Winners!

In March of 2021 we opened our second Biennial Open Fiction Contest. With so many great entries the decision was hard, but here are the winners. Our finalists were judged by Angela Jackson Brown, and we are indebted to her for her time.

First Place: *Funny Funny Fate* by Philip Walker
Second Place: *An American Love Story, 2006* by Sheila Mulrooney
Third Place: *Under Her Cellophane Skin* by Emily Jon Tobias

Honorable Mentions (*alphabetical by author*):
Hippos on the Aft Deck 6 by Sam Asher
A Survey of Modern Art by Elisa Faison
The Hypocrite by Robert Herbst

Philip Walker is a PhD student studying molecular biology who has recently developed a passion for writing.

First Place
Funny Funny Fate
Philip Walker

Angela says: *"Funny Funny Fate" was equal parts crime noir and philosophical fiction. The writer explores Death and the meaning of life but with a tongue in cheek approach that left me both smiling and contemplating the complexities of what I had just read. The main character of the story is searching for meaning, both of his life and of life in general, but in a way that doesn't feel preachy or contrived. The author plays with form and with multiple genres which makes for a riveting story. The ending is quite unexpected, and I found myself revisiting the story several times after my initial reading. I look forward to reading more from this author.*

On this particular morning I remembered what my mother told me before my first day of school.

"Don't be so nervous, Joseph. After all, what's the worst that could happen?" I had plenty of ideas. I could humiliate myself in front of the other children, I could get made fun of for the way I looked, or maybe nothing noteworthy would happen at all and I would live a miserable and unfulfilled life. There were so many good reasons to be afraid. I haven't changed much since that day, I'm still afraid of everything, all the time. It's quite exhausting really. Lately I've been thinking about how to change that, how to conquer my fears that have crippled me for so long, and today, I was finally going to try. Today I set out to conquer everyone's greatest fear, Death. Today was my first day as a contract killer.

I stepped outside to a beautiful morning in Buffalo, New York, and beautiful days in Buffalo were especially beautiful as they were so few and far between. My boss hadn't given me much instruction, other than to check my mailbox come Monday morning. When I did, I found three names written on the back of a napkin from the Blackbrick Diner, each name with a few personal descriptors and an address to lead me to the criminal. As I read the napkin, I started to think about all the things that could go wrong. What if I chickened out? What if I got caught and sent to jail for the rest of my life?

Then there was the best-case scenario: I murder three strangers. I do believe that good people can do terrible things under certain circumstances, and I hope that's what's happening here, though in such an unjust and unpleasant world, surely removing a few criminals was only a minor offence, if one at all. There's plenty of backstory to how I ended up a professional killer, but I don't like to dwell on the past anymore. Mine's not a very exciting one and I've heard it's not a particularly healthy thing to do. It's best to stay focused on the here and now. The task at hand. And today, that was William Schultz, who lived at 142 Bradford Avenue.'

CHAPTER 1: MR. WILLIAM SCHULTZ - THIEF, MURDERER, SCUMBAG - 142 BRADFORD AVENUE - APT 7B

There were plenty of thieves in the world, and surely most of them didn't deserve to die, however, William stole from powerful people and powerful people are reckless and unforgiving. Well, maybe people are reckless and unforgiving, but those with power seem to have the means to do some real damage.

I made my way up the fire escape of William's building before climbing into his one-bedroom apartment through the unlocked window. It was obvious nobody was here. There were books scattered on the floor, an antique record player on the coffee table, and one wooden chair in the middle of the living room pointed at the world's smallest television. After a quick look around, I already felt lost. Should I just wait for him? Should I move on to the next person? Maybe I just go home and forget this whole killing nonsense even crossed my mind. After some contemplation, I decided to not decide at all, and instead let fate make my decision for me. I was going to wait ten minutes and if William didn't show, I would leave and go back to my mundane life. It felt cowardly, letting the world dictate who and what I became. The whole point of doing this was to take control, experience, finally feel something. As I stood there on the tattered carpet second guessing my decision to not decide, the front door swung open abruptly. Unlike me, fate was decisive. And unfortunately for William, fate had chosen chaos.

As the door opened, I felt a jolt of adrenaline through my entire body. It was amazing. However, before I could even blink, William took an immediate left turn into the bathroom. He then quickly shut the door behind him, failing to even realize there was a stranger in his home. I thought it might have been a cool moment, sitting in another man's home, waiting for him in the dark with a loaded gun, then seeing that terrified look on his face as he opened the door. Maybe he would even drop his keys or spill a carton of milk like in the movies. Oh well. I was now listening to William the thief empty his bowels while I sat patiently in his living room, my sweaty hand tightly clutching the Kimber Deluxe Magnum Revolver I had bought yesterday. I looked down and noticed the price tag still on the grip panel. I quickly tore it off not to be embarrassed. William was now washing his hands. I took a deep breath. When he walked out and saw me, he remained calm. I tried my best to do the same, but I wasn't. I hope he didn't notice.

"Hi," he said.

"Hey," I replied, while steadying my aim on William's head.

"Are you here to kill me?" he asked.

William didn't seem confused but rather curious, as if having a stranger point a gun at him was an everyday occurrence and he was simply wondering who wanted him dead this time. He was annoyingly composed. Meanwhile, I was trying to figure out what to do with my hand that wasn't holding the gun. Should I put it in my pocket? Behind my back? Maybe I should just hold the gun with two hands. No, that would look weird. Murder was far more difficult than I anticipated. While I was deciding what to do with my off-hand, William moseyed into the kitchen and buried his head in the fridge. He grabbed an apple and started eating it as if I wasn't pointing a loaded gun at his brain. I finally put my hand in my back pocket and responded.

"Well, you're a thief."

"Yes. Did I steal something of yours?" As I shook my head no, he continued. "Then I suppose we aren't enemies, and you must be god punishing me for my sins," he said with a smile.

This is where it all went wrong. I should have never said *hey*. I should have never said anything at all. The more William spoke the harder it was for me to pull the trigger. He became more human with every word. How was I supposed to kill him after the effortless rapport we now shared? William once again asked me why I was here. I took a moment to really think about the question. A lifetime of boredom and regret? An appetite for some excitement in my miserable life? To be someone else completely? Someone who's actually lived.

"Your name was on a napkin," I said softly.

"Out of all the names in the world too, how unlucky."

I guess it was. I still didn't understand how William was so relaxed under the circumstances. His life was hanging in the balance, Death staring him square in the face, yet he didn't seem to care. Maybe he was too stupid to fully understand his position. The way you could hold a gun to a dog's head, and he might wag his tail and lick the barrel. It's also possible he just didn't care to live. Plenty of intelligent people have held that disposition before. Instead of spending the rest of my life wondering why William was the way he was, I decided to ask him.

"Everything happens for a reason my friend! The future is an unstoppable force unfolding before us uncontrollably. If you are meant to kill me I'm sure you will," he said with enthusiasm.

Ugh. William wasn't a fool or unhappy, he was an optimist. How depressing. He had a point though; things did constantly seem to happen without any rhyme or reason. The good and bad both coming and going as they please. I suppose everything could be boiled down to fate or luck one way or another. Sometimes I wonder what my life might be like had I caught a break or two. Maybe I had and could be even worse off than I already am. That seems unlikely though.

"What's your name?" he asked.

"Joseph." I'm not sure why I answered. I was sure murder wasn't supposed to involve so much dialogue, but it was nice to have someone to talk to, even under the circumstances. William was now digging through the pantry as he continued to equivocate about the meaning of life and death. He asked me if anyone had ever held a gun to my head, or if my life had ever flashed before me in fear of my own demise. He asked me how I could possibly take a life having never stared Death in the face.

"And you have?" I replied.

"Why of course. I've met Death so many times that we're good friends by now."

"Must be nice," I accidentally said aloud.

"What do you mean?"

"It must be nice to have a friend, especially one who visits often."

William laughed. He then continued rambling optimistic nonsense about the future. While William was well-spoken, he wasn't a man of great substance. He seemed too jovial to be a criminal. In fact, he seemed like a bit of an idiot. I suppose those are the most dangerous idiots though, the well-spoken ones. He wanted to know what my boss had told me about him and why he was to be killed. I had no idea. All I had was the napkin and the napkin said William was a thief, murderer, and a scumbag.

"I can't be a scumbag!" he shouted. I suppose that was him admitting to thieving and murdering. "Scumbags run the world. Do I look like a man in charge of anything?"

He didn't, and now William had done it. I couldn't kill him anymore. He was no longer just a name, he was William. Cool and calm, completely bizarre William. A man without fear and full of passion. A man who had probably lived an interesting and compelling life. I was full of admiration and envy. Those feelings often came together for me. I envied everything I admired. I think that's why it's been so difficult for me to enjoy this life.

"So, you're lonely then? Must be difficult getting to know people when you're holding a gun to their head," William said with a smirk.

"Sorry, I've actually never done this before."

"First day jitters? I can help with that you know."

"How do you figure?"

"I've killed plenty of people. I can teach you the art of taking a life. Is there another person you need to kill?"

"Yes, two others actually."

"Busy day. Well, we should take care of them first, by then you'll be an expert and dispense of me without a care. And then I can visit my old friend Death once again."

I didn't know what to say. William was a charming man and I wanted him to like me. I took a second to think about his offer.

". . . OK," I replied.

William smiled. "Excellent! So, who are we killing first?"

CHAPTER 2: MISS ELIZABETH HADDOCK - MURDERER, LIAR - 78 HAWTHORNE BAY

When we arrived at Miss Haddocks house it was apparent her sins were far more financially rewarding than William's. She lived in an upscale neighbourhood, one of the ones where every house on every block has freshly cut grass, perfectly shaped bushes, and multiple new shiny cars in their driveway. The type of neighbourhood that people drive through as an escape, just to imagine a better life. As we approached Elizabeth's front door, William wasted no time picking the cylinder lock with a misshapen paperclip he pulled from his torn cargo pants. When we entered, there was a packed suitcase and purse sitting beside the door, as if Miss Haddock was about to leave town. The luggage made my mind wander to all the places I'd rather be right now. A warm beach sipping a cocktail, hiking through lush mountains or a vast desert, sipping over-priced coffee at a small café in a city whose name I couldn't properly pronounce. Those are things people enjoy, right? I was never able to travel far from home while my father was ill and had always convinced myself that the rest of the world was just more of the same. Buildings, roads, people, little sprinkles of nature here and there.

As we moved past the foyer, I could see Elizabeth quietly eating dinner alone. She sat at the head of a dining table that was fit for a large family. I could only see the back of her head, but it was enough to see she was troubled. I wasn't good at much, but I could recognize displeasure as well as anyone. Elizabeth seemed even more displeased when William and I tied her to a chair and held a gun to her head. Her reaction was more of what I was expecting. A bit of fear and anger, but mostly panic. She, of course, wanted to know why we needed her dead. She denied being a murderer, but the napkin said she was a liar too so that was to be expected. William was now walking me through the process of killing Miss Haddock as she hyperventilated in the background. My first instinct was to shoot her in the head as it would be quick and painless for her, but when I lifted the gun and placed it between her eyes William let out an unapproving groan.

"What?" I asked.

William advised against shooting Elizabeth in the head, claiming it would be far too messy. That made sense. My second instinct was to ask Miss Haddock where she would like to be shot, however, William didn't like that either.

"No Joseph, you have to be decisive!" he said firmly.

"OK fine. I'm going to shoot her in the chest," I replied with confidence.

"Good. Then what?"

I was back to being confused. "...Then she'll be dead."

"Sure, but then what? Are you just going to walk away? What about the body? If someone finds her dead on the carpet with a bullet in her chest, they'll know she was murdered and start an investigation. You need to make it look like she could have just left town. You'll need to tidy up any blood or debris and dispose of the body."

This was starting to sound like an ordeal. I didn't know how to clean up blood or dispose of a body. William asked Elizabeth if she had any large garbage bags in the house that we could borrow, but she claimed to only have small kitchen bags. I suggested to William we quickly run to the store and grab some supplies before pulling the trigger. Elizabeth laughed.

"Go to the store? In the middle of a murder? I'm going to die at the hands of two idiots. Just put some blankets down, wrap up the body and dump it in the river you morons," she said in frustration.

William was impressed. "Now that's a killer! Quick on her feet and adaptable." He then rushed upstairs to grab some sheets that we could wrap Elizabeth's bloody corpse in. Meanwhile, Elizabeth and I shared an uncomfortable silence. As we shared that silence, I noticed just how beautiful Elizabeth was. I didn't really think about it at first, but she was. She had a narrow frame with short blonde hair, big bold green eyes, pale lips, and a sharp dainty nose. How was I going to kill her? She also had great breasts. I definitely couldn't kill her. Elizabeth eventually broke our silence to mock me on the way I was holding my revolver.

"Have you ever even held a gun before?" she asked with derision.

I had. A few times actually. When I was younger, I found a Kimber Deluxe .357 Magnum Revolver just like the one I had bought yesterday. My dad was a hunter and always had guns lying around our garage. There were certainly enough that he wouldn't notice if one were missing. I was fascinated by the weapon, so I decided to bring it up to my room. I kept it safe in my bottom dresser drawer, between my stash of sour patch kids and my Archie comic books. While most days it would sit there collecting dust, there were some days when I felt truly empty, without hope or want, and on those days, I would load one bullet into the six-shot chamber and spin it shut. Then, I would take a deep breath, hold the barrel to my head and pull the trigger. I don't know why it helped but it did. I guess it felt like something bigger than me was keeping me here, for some reason. A reason that I just didn't understand yet but was still there. Maybe fate, maybe luck, maybe something else completely. Elizabeth started to notice me drifting off and continued to yell at me.

"Hello? Are you daydreaming? What's wrong with you? You must be the most incompetent in-over-your-head fool I've ever met. You clearly have no idea what you're doing, I mean Jesus Christ you can't even tie a knot."

The last part of her rant caught my attention, but before I could react, Elizabeth freed her arms from the rope and shot up to her feet. She then pulled a pistol from her ankle and pointed it at me.

"You carry a gun in your own home?" I shouted.

She ordered me to drop my revolver, so I did. She then asked who I was working for. I would have told her if I knew but I didn't. Before she could interrogate me further, William snuck back downstairs with a pistol of his own. He ordered Elizabeth to lower her weapon.

"William! You had a gun this whole time too?" I asked.

"We're criminals Joseph, we have guns," he calmly replied.

William looked happy for me as he pressed his gun against the back of Elizabeth's neck.

"How was it?" he asked. "Having a gun pointed at you. Having your life hang in the balance. It's exhilarating, isn't it? Did you see him? Did you see Death?"

I said I did to satisfy William, but I didn't. It had all happened so fast. What a disappointment. Elizabeth reluctantly lowered her weapon and slunk back into her chair while William followed. William then looked at me and smiled.

"What an exciting day this has been. One minute you're the predator, and the very next you're the prey. Life sure is funny sometimes, isn't it? How you can almost always expect the unexpected. This all reminds me of a poem I wrote the first time I saw Death. Would you like to hear it?"

Neither Elizabeth nor I responded but William continued with his poem anyway. It went like this:

The Germans are coming the Germans are near
They march over hills while we tremble in fear
The Germans are coming the Germans are near
Their will absolute and hatred sincere

The Germans are coming the Germans are near
I rushed to my tent to hide from despair
The Germans are coming the Germans are near
The smell of men dying is rich in the air

The Germans are coming the Germans are near
I hear German boots approaching my lair
The Germans are coming the Germans are near
He opened the door and saw me stood there

A German is coming a German is near
His eyes full of dread and mine full of tears
Life sure is funny a German is here
He lowered his weapon I poured him a beer

William lowered his gun and suggested we spare Elizabeth's life. "We're all soldiers, Joseph. I don't think we need to be killing each other."

I looked down at Elizabeth and she looked up at me like a child asking their mother for ice cream. I already knew I couldn't kill her. She was far too attractive and sad.

"OK," I said.

William was pleased. "That's excellent because I've found a painting worth a great deal of money upstairs in the bedroom. I suggest Elizabeth give us the papers of authenticity in exchange for her life."

William was now sporting a cheeky grin as his sympathetic change of heart was starting to make sense. Clearly William favored thieving over murdering. While Elizabeth was more than willing to give us the painting in exchange for not being murdered, I was now feeling more hopeless than ever. This day was supposed to go differently. This life was supposed to go differently. I didn't really care about the money, I just wanted to kill somebody. The thrill, the adrenaline. I had only gotten a taste so far and wanted the whole thing. What could make you feel more alive than to watch someone die? To take their life with your own hands? Nevertheless, I agreed to the deal as long as both William and Elizabeth would help me kill the last name on the list. Elizabeth was reluctant but didn't really have a choice.

"Who's the last person?" she asked.

I showed her the napkin."

CHAPTER 3: JAVIER JUAN ESTEBAN RODRIGO DE LA CRUZ III - PSYCHOPATH - THE BLACKBRICK DINER

The Blackbrick diner was past city limits and essentially in the middle of nowhere. When we arrived, the dining area was mostly empty besides a young couple sharing a corner booth and an old man eating soup up at the counter. We decided to order food while we thought up a way to find and kill the last target. Attempted murder was hungry work. William couldn't help but make conversation when we sat down, asking Elizabeth why she thought her name was on the napkin in the first place. Elizabeth was a contract killer like me, only successful. She had been killing for years now but had officially retired just a week ago. It's why she had her bags packed and waiting in the foyer.

"I'm headed to the Golden State, California!" she said with excitement. "A childhood friend of mine moved there last year and sends me beautiful postcards of the scenery every month. She says every day is full of sunshine. There's the ocean, mountains, beaches, deserts, parks, everything beautiful about the world in one place. I'll be staying in wine country just outside the Sonoma County, which is North of all the big cities. I've already found myself work at a small vineyard just five kilometers from the water. Every day when the sun sets it falls beneath the endless ocean, then in the mornings it ascends above the green Mayacamas mountains. It's going to be a brand new and honest life for me, one without crime, without death, and full of joy. The way a life is meant to be lived."

Elizabeth had a twinkle in her eye while telling us her plans and even showed us her one-way ticket to San Francisco. It sounded appealing, starting fresh in a brand-new place. I had never been west of Michigan myself. Our waiter soon interrupted to take our orders. I asked for a ham and swiss sandwich with no tomatoes, a side of shredded hash browns and pork sausage. I then asked to substitute my toast for a side house salad, but that's when our waiter grabbed a silver Ruger from his apron and pressed it to my forehead.

"Just the toast is fine too," I said nervously.

"Why aren't these two dead, Joseph?" he asked.

This was Javier. He was apparently the man who hired me and the man who wanted William and Elizabeth dead. He had put his own name on the napkin to ensure I would come find him so he could kill me himself to cover his tracks. William was impressed.

"Well thought out, Javier!" William shouted.

The story goes that William had stolen merchandise from Javier's family who ran a drug cartel, and Elizabeth had killed Javier's uncle on a job. I suppose Javier's biggest gripe was with Elizabeth as he moved the gun from my head to hers. He then ordered all of us to put our weapons on the table. We did. By this time, the young couple had made a quick exit, but the old man stayed seated at the counter eating his soup. With Javier's attention still focused on Elizabeth, William grabbed his gun from the table and pointed it at Javier. In response, Javier grabbed Elizabeth by the neck and threatened to kill her if William didn't drop his gun. I sat and watched.

I wasn't sure what to do. I looked around the room. My life was now completely upside down. There was chaos, excitement, everything I wanted. Still, I felt as if nothing had changed at all. Still lost and confused, still indifferent towards it all. I looked around for something, anything to live for, but I couldn't find it. Not even something to die for. The only thing that caught my eye was that old familiar Kimber Magnum Deluxe that laid in front of me on the tabletop, so I picked it up. Javier threatened to shoot me if I didn't put it down, but he didn't. Fate I suppose. Elizabeth and William were confused but I wasn't anymore. I had finally made a decision. I lifted the revolver and pressed it to my temple like I had so many times as a young man, however, this time it was different. I closed my eyes and time stood still. When I opened them again, he was there. Death. Staring at me while I trembled in front of him.

"Hi," he said.

"Hey," I replied.

He mentioned the beautiful weather we'd been having. I agreed, the weather had been nice. He then looked down and read from his napkin.

"You're Joseph McKinley, right? Timid, coward, loser, lives at 48 Belmont Road?"

"Ya, that's me."

Without a second of doubt, he raised his scythe to strike me down. I was underwhelmed.

"That's it? This was supposed to be revelatory, not small talk" I said.

"Sorry, busy times. Death doesn't rest."

"That's sad. Don't you get tired? Always working, always killing?"

"Yes. And thank you for asking. Nobody ever asks about Death."

"No problem. Well, I wouldn't want to keep a busy man."

Death raised his scythe again, but I interrupted once more.

"Wait, Death. I thought my life was supposed to flash before my eyes?"

"Oh, did it not? Hmm, you must not have any particularly noteworthy memories."

"Oh. Yeesh, OK."

Death looked at me with pity. "That's not a very nice way to die, having never even lived. Tell you what, you go make some memories and next time I come, we can enjoy them together one last time. Deal?"

"Deal," I replied.

Death was nice. Certainly, nicer than most people, and certainly no one to fear. I was back in the diner now. It seemed as if a lot had happened since I drifted off as William and I were the only ones left alive. Javier and Elizabeth were both lying in a pool of their own blood on the dusty checkered tile. Javier's cold hand still clutching his silver Ruger, his dead body covering most of Elizabeth's. I could only see a few strands of her vanilla blonde hair and blood slowly dripping down that sharp dainty nose. I assume Javier had shot Elizabeth and William had subsequently shot Javier, but I couldn't be sure. The old man was dead too, but I couldn't begin to tell you how that happened. Maybe an unlucky stray bullet, maybe the unstoppable force of fate. I placed my revolver back down on the counter and spotted Elizabeth's ticket sticking out from her blouse. As I grabbed the ticket from her mangled corpse, I felt a brand-new sense of optimism. I stood up tall and headed for the exit, as I had some living to do. Unfortunately, before I could make it out the door William stopped me.

"I can't just let you leave after everything that's happened today, Joseph," he said bluntly.

He then tossed his empty pistol aside, picked my revolver off the counter, and held it to my chest. Like a real killer, he pulled the trigger without hesitation. There was a deafening bang, but no bullet fired. He tried again and again but still nothing. He then held up the gun to further inspect it and started to laugh.

Fate is a funny thing. You can find it in sparing a woman's life only to see her murdered moments later. Or my father fighting cancer for a decade only to be killed by a brain aneurysm two months into remission. And you'll even find it in an ill-equipped killer accidentally buying a cap gun instead of a real functioning revolver.

"I wonder what it is," William said curiously.

"What's that?" I asked.

"I wonder what it is fate's been keeping us around for."

I had no idea, but I intended on finding out. William and I shook hands and went our separate ways. Him with the painting, me with the ticket. My first order of business was to watch the sun fall beneath the ocean and rise above the mountains.

On my way to the airport, I thought of a poem. It went like this:

Funny funny life
Funny funny fate
Giving us things
Just to take them away

Bring me up high
Bring me down low
The rain in the storm
The pretty rainbow

Funny funny Death
Look at you go
Giving me life
Giving me hope

Hope just for now
Until comes the day
You find a clever way
To take it all away

Funny funny luck
How silly you are
Giving me light
While another goes dark

Funny funny fate
Now sunshine awaits
I bet that I die
On the plane on the way

Sheila Mulrooney *(she/her) is the lead editor of Autofocus, a publisher of artful autobiographical writing. Her work has been nominated for Best of Small Fictions and appeared in publications such as Barnstorm Journal, Lost Balloon, and elsewhere. You can find her on twitter at @SJosephine10.*

Second Place
An American Love Story, 2006
Sheila Mulrooney

Angela says: "An American Love Story, 2006" explores race, politics, and class but in such a way that it leaves the reader contemplating exactly how they should view both the characters and the plot. I found myself questioning so many things about the story and my interpretation of it. I love when this happens when reading new stories because it means the writer left space for the reader. I hope to read more by this author.

He was waiting for his older brother Javier to drop off the weed. Normally they kept these transactions quick. But tonight they were selling to a bunch of Berkley students—white girls who wore eyeliner and danced to music with a strong bass. They arranged to meet at a campus bar with fruity drinks, and he tried a strawberry lemonade vodka while Javier went out back. That's when he met Helen.

She had a tight blond ponytail and cowgirl boots, a sophomore studying environmental science. He said he was a senior in English.

"You won't make any money in English. Who's gonna pay you to know about books?"

"You never know. I might write the next great American novel and make millions."

"What would you write about?"

"English majors. And all the people who doubted them."

She laughed, a harsh sound exploding from her, even though the joke was bad. He liked that; he smiled.

"I'm only kidding," he said. "Obviously I'd write about you."

#

He had known her a month when he had to lay his motorcycle down. It was on a backwater highway, the exit before his mother's ranch house. He was merging right as an eighteen-wheeler switched lanes. It was either the slide or his legs. Afterwards he was fine—just scrapes all up his body and a ruined leather jacket. The bike was trashed, but he managed to scrap it for a couple hundred.

"Too bad," said Javier. "That thing was a chick magnet. And cheap as hell too."

By winter he was a regular on public transit and missed the bike. Not riding it so much—the accident had terrified him. Instead, he missed how the bike made him feel: American, edging towards some promise of freedom. Wilderness, the frontier. On the bike, he could take a day and ride to Oregon. Go to Nevada, gamble in Las Vegas, pick up Javier's weed and take a cut of whatever it sold for.

One summer he crossed the southern border to visit his mother's hometown. He didn't stay long. He found it odd, almost criminal, to stand in the place his family had left.

#

He used the money from the motorcycle to buy Helen dinner. Her father was a military man, a conservative, so he chose a place with tablecloths and a wine list. He held open the door and said she looked nice. Once they sat down, he asked about her classes, mostly because it was the only thing he could think of.

"They're filled with bleeding hearts," she said airily. "Everyone's so concerned about endangered species. As if species haven't been dying since the dawn of time."

"You don't think we should try saving some? If we can?"

She shook her head. He noticed she seemed completely relaxed, unphased by the nice restaurant, his button-down shirt. This bothered him.

"For every species that dies, a hundred new ones come to life. Maybe they're not as cute as pandas but," she shrugs. "This is science. We're not here to be cute."

He was surprised that he agreed with her. He thought it was smart, the sort of thing no one ever said. He walked her home and fingered her in her apartment stairwell. She didn't come at first, but she kept muttering instructions. *Do it softer, I'm not wet enough, yes that's better, yes good yes.*

#

It wasn't like he was the campus heartthrob, but he was good at women. His leather jacket helped, and his features were much lighter than his siblings. Hazel eyes, fine hair, arched eyebrows. He inherited the Portuguese on his father's side, none of the indigenous Mexican from his mother. The only truly Hispanic thing about him was his leg hair, sprouting in black gnarls, and how much he sweat. In buckets, under any sun. Whenever he could, he took off his shirt. This also helped with girls.

"White women love him," complained Javier. "They're not scared he's peddling drugs or has a gun. They jump into his arms."

"It's also because he studies English," said Rose, their sister. "College is the one place sensitive guys are cute. Anywhere else, they're useless."

Rose was right. He knew that and he took advantage of it. His lectures were filled with pretty women, brunettes with light eyes and quirky laughs, who were generally insecure. Mostly they moved in groups, but occasionally there was a girl who would sit alone and take diligent notes. He was best with this demographic. A casual approach, easy chatter, an interesting point about Pynchon or Kerouac. They would sleep with him for weeks, inviting him to spend the weekend so he wouldn't have to commute home.

#

On their fourth date, he took her to BAMPFA. A cubist exhibition was visiting, and students got in free. Around them stood groups of twos and threes, well dressed women with shiny blouses and men with ironed shirts. Helen spoke too loudly, her voice cutting through the murmur of whispers. This embarrassed him, but he also felt strangely defensive of her.

"This painting looks like shapes," she said. "Like a kindergarten class learning primary colors."

He paused for a moment, as if considering this, then said, "What about the balance?"

She did not respond, so he stepped closer and lowered his voice, in part because it was seductive, but also because she might imitate his hushed tone.

"When you look at it, you expect the shapes to line up a certain way. To make geometrical sense. But the more you look, the more you see that the shapes defy you at the last second. They won't do what you want."

Helen crossed her arms and shifted her weight to one leg. He noticed, not for the first time, how wide her hips were. Crescent moons that moved when she walked. If she hadn't been frowning, he would have touched her.

"Maybe I'm missing it," she admitted after a minute. "It's in a museum after all."

He thought he had won a point. It wasn't often she allowed for misinterpretation on her side. He was discovering that normally Helen stuck to her guns, disagreed to the point of stupidity. He was still reveling in this victory when she caught glance of a Kandinsky in the next room and snorted loudly. A middle-aged woman threw them a dirty look. Helen did not notice, but he blushed.

#

When he was seven, his father flung himself off a building. The scaffolding of a building, really. He had been on the job, construction for a new housing unit. One of the thousand apartment complexes that now blocked the beach front. He described the way his father fell to Helen. Like a black bird in a nosedive. Something cracked when he finally hit the pavement.

"Wow, I'm sorry," she said. "I didn't know." She stayed silent for a moment then asked, "Why were you there?"

At her question a breath caught in his throat. No one had ever asked that before; he'd almost forgotten why. Then he began to talk. He told Helen about his father's depression, the twenty-hour shifts he worked in construction and landscaping, trying to feed ten children.

"Ten," she repeated, eyes widening. "An immigrant family with ten?"

"Catholics," he shrugged. "No contraception. It's just what you do."

He was the second youngest. Javier was two years older, Rose one year. His little brother had died as a baby. Malnutrition. Nobody fed him, and he slept in a shoebox. The rest were older, he didn't know by how much. His eldest brother, Benjamin, had moved away and sent money home for their mother and his tuition.

"Rose and I were the babies, so we couldn't be left alone. Every day after school my older sister Maria would walk us to my dad's construction site. It was on the way to the diner where she waitressed. Then Rose and I would wait at the foreman's trailer until Dad was done. In winter we'd wait inside, do our homework or whatever. But when it was warm, we'd hang out on the steps. Build houses from rocks or play tag or something. We could see the construction workers, but we never really paid attention to them. The day he jumped I was facing the building because we were playing hide and seek, and my hiding place had me crouched underneath the trailer. I saw a crowd of men on one floor, then one of them fall. I only found out it was Dad the next day. The foreman walked us home, didn't hint at anything. Said Dad had to work late, and that was it."

She touched him after that, softly. It was the most tenderness she had ever showed. Normally she was very down to business in bed, required almost no warming up. He liked that; she came quickly. But when her finger brushed his cheek, he was surprised to see it was wet. He had been crying.

#

The next week was the first time he cheated. It wasn't like he was planning it. But it was so easy, he felt it would be wrong to say no.

He was in the library looking for a book of Emerson essays. He wanted Helen to read it. He thought she would like "Self-Reliance" and "Experience," all the astrological metaphors. But he hadn't found it and settled for Thoreau instead. He was already late to meet her.

"Life in the woods, huh?" said the librarian. She smiled. "You don't really seem like the type."

He looked her up and down. She had blue eyes, short hair that curled behind her ears. Tassels lined her sleeves, and a stem of baby's breath was tattooed on her wrist. Suddenly he was hyperaware of the library's emptiness, just before closing.

"Why not?" he asked. "Think a bear would eat me?"

She grinned. Her name was Nicole; she was an MA student writing on Faulkner and Shirley Jackson.

"*The Lottery,* right? Are you into systemized murder?"

"Her commentary on government oppression is actually brilliant," she said. "It's such shit people only know that one story. I can show you some of her better stuff. After I re-shelve these books, I'm free."

Later he recounted everything to Javier, who laughed and laughed. His favorite part was that he didn't even miss the date with Helen. He was only an hour late. When her roommates let him in, he found her curled on her bed wearing sweatpants. She was in the middle of a nap.

#

Two-timing was less stressful than he thought. He only met Nicole in the library after hours. That left the evening for Helen. When Helen asked what he'd done that day, he'd always shrug and say he was in the library, studying.

Javier thought it was hilarious. He even insisted on seeing Nicole. One day he had a deal on campus, and afterwards they hovered around the library until she showed up.

"She's cute," Javier said. "Damn cute. Why don't you ditch Helen and date her? What are you still with the blond for anyway?"

He had asked himself the same question, more than once. It wasn't just for sex, although that was huge; he would be stupid to ignore that. There was something about going from one woman to another, a secret passageway entirely his own. He began to think of the commute from the library to Helen's as a canal, manmade and reliable, a hollowing out of something by his own hands, now flowing with pure, clean water.

#

After the holidays, they had their first fight. It was about ICE. Helen said it was reasonable, even necessary, to protect a country's borders, especially after 9/11. He said that was a fundamental misunderstanding of how governments mobilized nationalistic narratives. She rolled her eyes and said not everything was a story; some things actually existed and threatened the American people.

"Dirt poor Hispanics are not a threat to the American people. And anyone with eyes can see the deportation camps they're building are the real threat. You don't know what you're talking about," he continued, speaking over her. "Seriously Helen. You have no idea."

He was surprised by how hoarse his voice was. His hands were trembling, and he wanted to hit something. Smash Helen's mirror or punch her wall. He wasn't used to violence like this. If deals went badly, normally Javier did the fighting. The closest he had ever been to physical danger was the motorcycle accident, which since dating Helen he had not thought about very much.

She said she'd do some reading. They could talk about it later, when she knew more. This frustrated him. It was just like Helen not to concede immediately. He commuted home that night, even though she asked him to stay.

Nicole, he knew, agreed with him. She went to rallies about mistreatment of immigrants; she read people like Jonathan Franzen and would occasionally correct his terminology when they talked politics. As soon as she learned his last name, she understood. Sometimes she directed him towards different scholarships designated for Hispanics.

The funny thing was he did not care that Nicole agreed with him. It seemed monumentally irrelevant, like she had boarded a different bus in a different city. He cared about Helen. He cared that she said those things, that she thought them and might keep thinking them forever. Their entire relationship seemed tilted slightly, like she had amputated one of his legs and he only now realized that this changed his life permanently, altering the world so everything was unfamiliar and every movement required pain.

He explained all of this to Javier. Javier listened, then shrugged, and said something dismissive about white women and their politics.

"So you must be full-time with the librarian then? You're not still sleeping with Helen, are you?"

He hit the joint before answering. Yes. Yes, he was.

#

Things were different. They didn't go out anymore; they only argued and fucked. He began reading newspapers, circling articles for Helen. Nicole helped him find hard-hitting sections, points they considered irrefutable. She lent him pamphlets and paperbacks, books he had never heard of whose titles included phrases like *The Political Unconscious* and *Otherness in a Post-Liberal World*. He skimmed their pages and felt smarter, more alive. Like someone who was part of society.

Still, all he thought about was Helen—reaching her, being heard. They spent hours arguing, circling round each other late into the night. That labor camps were inhumane was her first admission. More followed, but they were normally buffeted with qualifications or questions. She didn't seem capable of believing that the government could destroy lives; she was stubborn, clinging to her vision of a paternalistic presence. Uncle Sam, who needed her.

"How can you buy that shit?" he asked desperately. "It's propaganda, some story they whip up for civilians."

She smiled and shook her head. "Not everything belongs in a novel. Some things are real."

He grew confused. He wanted to leave her, but he needed her. The sex was incredible. He began noticing her body in new ways—the sweat that pooled in the small of her back; the fat of her breasts spilling over her bra. She frustrated him, sexually and intellectually. He never lasted long on the nights they talked politics, but neither did she.

#

One evening they watched *Crossing Arizona.* It was another recommendation from Nicole. She'd never seen it, but her professor said it was "a devastating critique." The New York Times had called it "a triumph."

Things were going well with Nicole. They still only met in the library, but they talked more now, about their lives as well as politics and literature. He'd even told her about Helen—not their sleeping together, but her beliefs. How they hurt him.

"It feels like she's incomplete sometimes, you know? Like she should agree with me about this stuff, but she just doesn't."

Nicole was re-shelving books. He could tell he had only half her attention, but this made it easier to speak. Like he could take back whatever he said, if he really wanted.

"It's nice of you to care so much," Nicole said. "But honestly I wouldn't bother. People like this aren't worth it."

That night, Helen cried at the movie, and he thought about how much he didn't want to lose her. What a waste it would all be, if she simply disappeared. She pressed her face into his shoulder, and he felt her warm tears soak through his shirt. His hands fluttered down her spine and he grasped the fat above each hip. He imagined pinching her, softly at first and then harder, until she cried out in pain.

He murmured *I love you* into her hair. It wasn't the first time he'd said it, but it was the first time he believed himself. She didn't seem to notice the difference.

#

In April they heard about the deportations. Congress debated whether to forgive illegals or invoke the Immigration Nationality Act. In Costa Mesa, a day laborer job center shut down, leaving hundreds of immigrants without work. The police were being trained to pursue and retain.

"Will your mother be okay?" asked Nicole. "It's climbing up the coast, fast."

"Nah," he said. "It will take them at least a decade to get through Las Vegas. We won't have to worry about anything until 2016."

Nicole said he needed to get a job. She began scheduling meetings for him. 'Informational interviews' with people in journalism, communications, sales.

"They won't deport you if you're making money," she said grimly.

Javier and Rose seemed to agree. Javier stopped dealing, 'temporarily,' and began stocking shelves at the local supermarket. Rose picked up extra shifts at the seamstress, moving her classes to the night section.

"We'll be fine," Rose assured him. "We're anchor babies, Bush can't touch us."

Still, everyone worried. Recruiters heard his last name and their eyes glazed over. Rose and Javier were not home as much, and when they were, they slept. Almost no one drank anymore, and Javier had even given up smoking. Only Helen remained unchanged. Unaffected, as if the crisis was just a piece of trivia, another story on the news. He began to think that the air in her house was cleaner somehow, different than the dense anxiety constantly surrounding him.

He could not stop himself. He went over whenever he could. He was drawn to her with such force, he felt strong, almost invincible. They could deport him anytime they wanted, he told himself. It wouldn't do anything. He would always come right back.

#

Rose threw a graduation party. He wished she wouldn't, it wasn't the right time, there was too much going on, and besides he didn't have a job yet, so what did graduating really matter?

"Being a student is a job," said Rose coldly. "And nothing cheers people up like a party."

She and Javier cleared out the backyard, strung Christmas lights through tree branches. Maria lent them picnic tables from the restaurant she managed, and the other siblings pooled their cash for hard alcohol, fruit, and beer. Benjamin said he would come to town.

"Invite Helen," Rose told him. "I want to meet her."

He invited Helen, and he did not invite Nicole. This seemed very significant to him, like the beginning of a choice.

"You're making a mistake," said Javier. "Nicole will stick around for longer. She knows who you are. This Helen chick—you're just chasing some schoolboy crush. It's like you're trying to bang a kindergarten teacher but haven't followed the rules. Waste of time."

He wondered if he agreed, then finished Javier's joint. It was the last of his weed. His dealer was south, near the border, so he'd stopped going for a while. They both watched curls of smoke rise from his mouth solemnly.

A moment later Javier said, "But you know what the really good thing about this party will be? The dough. Rose has invited every relative of ours in the state. They're gonna pound you with so many checks, you won't know what to do with yourself."

#

The night before the party the news ran a story about raids in Southern California. *More than 700 immigrations netted,* one headline read. *Officers detain on site.* The operation was dubbed *Return to Sender.* The TV played clips of two men who were sex offenders. A newscaster said over 2,000 illegals were arrested in total.

He and Nicole followed the story all day, talking over each other without looking away from the screen. He could tell they were experiencing the same thing. A kind of exhilaration, almost giddiness, that the occasion they had dreaded, waited for, was actually happening. It felt like he was a puppet with all his strings cut loose. Limp, unable to move himself, but finally vindicated, exposed for being the exact thing he was.

#

He remembers that she looked nice the night of the party. She wore a white dress with a ruffled skirt and halter neckline. Something was different about her hair. It was smoother, cascading past her collarbone down to her breasts. He watched as she walked up his driveway and imagined pouring cold water over her, so the white fabric turned translucent and clung to her flesh.

She smiled when he said she looked beautiful. "I figured I'd better. Meeting the family and everything."

She looked at him from beneath her eyelashes. It was unusually coquettish for her, he thought, and this bothered him. Had he wanted this version of Helen, done up and flirtatious? It seemed odd that she was attempting to seduce him this way, by such crude means, when for the past six months he only longed for her good opinion and her approval—her sanction that he had a right to exist, and a right to exist with her.

"I'll get a job," he blurted out without thinking. "I promise."

They were outside his backyard now, hidden by a cluster of sagebrush. He could hear Rose's laugh, the thick accents of his older siblings. He positioned himself between Helen and the party, forcing her into the plants so no one would see them. He felt slightly insane. He had the wild urge to strip her dress from her, or run down the street, ride the next bus to the end of its line.

"That makes sense," she said, bemused. "Everyone needs a job at some point."

"But if I get a job will you live with me?" He stepped closer to her. "I don't want you to leave me, Helen. I love you."

All this sounded very pat to him, as if he was delivering lines from a poorly written TV show. He wished he had some better way of expressing himself—a line from Emerson or John Wayne, maybe. But those were the words that tumbled out of him because, he supposed later, they must be true.

She was staring at him, confused. Had he gone too far, he wondered. Would she finally laugh at him, turn around and leave the party, call him dirty, worthless, illegal? He studied her face, willing himself to remember everything about it, in case he never saw her again. But he was distracted by the powdered blush caked onto her cheeks. It was too much makeup, girlish and insincere. He wanted to tell her this. Then she leaned forward and kissed him, wrapping her arms around his waist.

"I was trying to figure out if you were drunk," she whispered. "I wouldn't say yes if you were, in case you forgot tomorrow. But I think you're sober, so yes."

He hugged her back, squeezing her into his shirt. He felt taller somehow, inflated with belief. He did not bother telling her that he was high.

#

"Where's Javier?"

He shrugged, not looking at Rose. They were leaning against the punch table, outside the periphery of the party. He watched as Helen chatted with his cousins and Benjamin. Her white dress seemed golden under the strings of lights. She is beautiful, he thought. She is mine.

"I'm serious, he was supposed to be home two hours ago."

"He's probably high, give him another hour and he'll be here."

"The car's been gone since yesterday." She nudged him, saying his name in a low voice. "I'm worried. What if he went south for weed and ran into the cops?"

Immediately images from yesterday's news reels flashed across his mind. One journalist managed to interview a detainee. A middle-aged woman with saggy arms. She was crying, saying that they had no toilet paper. *700 immigrants netted. Return to sender.*

"He's fine," he said flatly. He turned and grabbed himself another beer. "We're anchor babies, remember? They can't touch us."

These were Rose's words. He repeated them to make her feel better. Rose smiled, but he could tell it had not worked. They were both thinking the same thing. At this point, anything could be touched. Their last name was all the officers needed to know.

He glanced over his shoulder at Helen. She had not moved, holding her beer and laughing at something Benjamin said. She was beautiful.

#

The party was dying. Javier had not yet come. Helen was drunk, her breath thick with beer and she dozed off quietly on his chest, her legs curled beneath her like a schoolgirl. Rose had gone inside to clean dishes.

She was right to throw the party, he thought. He would thank her later. But now, a strange pall had cast itself over him, the weed, the alcohol, Helen's body all twisting together like sheets in a bed that was not his own. Part of him felt he was suffocating, but if he was, it was by perfumed silk, something fine and rare. Then he heard Javier's voice through the kitchen window.

"The bastard who towed us tried to charge three-fifty. We were damn lucky I had some on me."

A high-pitched laugh drowned what he said next. Then Rose called his name. Slowly he extracted himself from Helen, guiding her head so she slept on the picnic table, her face buried in her arms.

"Where are you going?" she murmured. "Will you come back?"

He said yes and kissed her hair. The scent of her stayed with him as he stepped over crushed red cups and empty beer cans, and he savored it, teasing himself with thoughts of her white dress, her wide hips. He would leave after this, he decided. Yell at Javier for worrying Rose, then disappear into the night with Helen.

Inside, Rose was hunched over the sink, scrubbing dishes clean. Behind her stood Javier and a small girl with a tasseled coat. It was Nicole.

"Congratulations!" she cried, flinging herself on him. Her lips brushed his cheek. They felt chapped but smelled like vanilla. "It was supposed to be a surprise. But now we've missed the party."

Javier and Nicole told the whole story. How Javier had found her in the library, invited her as a 'present' for him. They arranged that he would drive uptown to get her, but the car crapped out, it was a piece of shit anyway. The night before Javier had been down south to pick up a few pounds for the party, but still nowhere near the raids. All the driving fucked up the tires, that's why they were late, they had to get a tow.

Nicole kept stroking his arm. She was high and drunk, he realized. Javier loved doing that whenever someone drove with him; he considered offering his passengers drugs a sign of hospitality.

It was less painful than he expected. Nicole was still holding him when Helen came inside. He introduced them, staring at his shoes as he did, and Nicole said, "Helen, nice to meet you. I hear you've been talking politics with my man."

There was a pause. Then Helen said, "Sorry, I didn't realize he was yours."

Rose was the one who saved him. She offered to call Helen a cab or lend her change for the bus. They stepped out of the kitchen together. What expression Helen wore he did not see. He never looked up from his shoes.

#

He got just under a grand from his graduation party, most of it from Benjamin. He used the money to buy a secondhand motorcycle. When Rose asked where he would go, he shrugged and said something about the Midwest, maybe Canada. Somewhere with cold winters, real seasons, not like California. Somewhere people had never seen a Hispanic immigrant.

"But how will you pay rent? And won't you be lonely?"

"Nah. I'll work on the next great American novel," he joked. "Next time you see me I'll be world famous."

He did not mean that of course. What he really meant was that he was already lonely. Like he had somehow stumbled into the wrong exam room and now had to fill white booklets with information he did not know. Once when he was very young his father brought home a book of Spanish poetry. It was *Primero Sueño*, by Sor Juana. His father did not know who she was; he only knew the book was in Spanish and ninety-nine cents in the bargain bin.

"For you," he said. "Open it. Read to me."

He tried, but his accent was poor. He had only attended English-speaking schools. He tripped over the tildes, and his "a"s were too flat. He read a page or two, then paused, hoping his father would let him stop. When he looked up, his father shook his head, muttering something in Spanish. To this day, he's not sure what it was.

He leaves the next morning, early. No one stops him as he crosses the state borderline. He has the strange feeling that he does not exist.

Emily Jon Tobias (she/her) received her MFA in Writing from Pacific University Oregon and her bachelor's degree in creative writing from the University of Wisconsin Milwaukee. Her work has appeared in literary journals such as Santa Clara Review, Talking River Review, Flying South Literary Journal, Furrow Literary Journal, The Opiate Magazine, The Ocotillo Review, and Jerry Jazz Musician, among others. Currently, she is a 2022 Pushcart nominee.

Third Place
Under Her Cellophane Skin
Emily Jon Tobias

Angela says: "Under Her Cellophane Skin" explores homelessness among teenagers – an aspect of society that we often try to avoid discussing or facing, but the author did so in a thoughtful and humane manner. I found myself silently rooting for the main character who is initially referred to as only "that girl." Well, the author was able to make "that girl" represent any girl who happened to have a series of unfortunate events happen to her. I found the prose engaging and the ultimate end of the story believable. "Under Her Cellophane Skin" is one of those stories the reader will remember long after reading the final word. I am hoping I get to read more by this author.

That girl there. With an empty bottle in a brown paper bag at her side. She's missing. Been reported by her father. Legs wide, sprawled on a blue plastic tarp under the overhang of Union Gospel Mission, the men's shelter down from the 7-Eleven against Skid Row. She's been spare-changing around Pioneer Square all morning. Did well enough to have nodded out by noon, chin resting against her chest. This is her usual spot.

On the street, a rush of warmth comes over the girl. She's under the shelter of an old man standing above her. He unzips his jacket—the one given to him upon retirement from the UW Science Department—royal purple with a UW emblem on its sleeve. He slides his arms out, then gently edges the girl's limp body forward to lay the jacket around her shoulders. Next, he reaches through the cuff of one sleeve to catch hold of her hand, feeding her arm through, as if clothing a child in winter. After he's finished tending to her arms, the man zips her up. Now, she's cocooned in the jacket with sleeves hanging way past her hands hiding the rig she'll pluck from her arm when she comes to.

Now, a sightseer, shuffling along in a cattle row to tour the Seattle underground, almost trips over her soiled legs. Nonchalant locals rush by the girl as if weaving around traffic cones. The homeless here are like street lights or sign posts, forgotten city fixtures. One says, God loves you, then tosses a handful of coins at her feet. Months living on Seattle streets. West Coast heroin is stronger than back home. They call it Hero on these streets, and she loves this, how Hero takes you over like Spider-Man to Peter Parker. The girl feels cradled in her coma, protected. Her Hero has conviction, gets her having visions during daylight hours. She swings from webs, walks on water. Hero helps her see the truth of things. It's all so beautiful, really, like gliding across the gates of heaven.

Today, Lemon sees her sister way up there, hovering. Lucy wears a summer dress, no . . . a nightgown, white cotton, with tiny berries embroidered along the collar . . . berries at each buttonhole down the front . . . berries along the dainty elastic edges of both ruffled cuffs. Her tangerine hair is washed and combed, sweeping through puddles along the street below her, wet and gathered at the ends like a paintbrush. Her feet are bare and unscathed as an infant's. She's *alive* and serene . . . beautiful, clean. Then Lucy is right above Lemon on the street and she whispers so close, so close, so close, she says, Don't forget you are fuchsia under all that black. Lemon tries to touch her face but the angel's body shrivels, turns in on itself, like a snail to salt, and suddenly, she's tasting the hardened creature on her tongue.

In front of her now, the old man bends to pick up coins scattered around the girl. He sets them in a neat pile beside her, then tunes his old AM/FM radio headphones. Jackson Browne, yes, that's it. Over the hood that's come down around her eyes, he places the headphones thoughtfully, like a tiara. Then, in a wave inside herself, Lemon feels her father here. Turning out the light beside her childhood bed, drawing the covers up toward her chin. Her father molds the edges of her small body until she's completely swaddled in soft down so that only her face shows and he can kiss her forehead and say, Close your eyes, Lemon. Go to sleep now, my girl. I love you.

The song softens, muffled by her matted red hair as the old man leaves her in a whole other place with music suctioned to her ears. *Running on empty* . . . a place of dusk and childhood on the Mississippi with her father. *Running blind* . . . on the river's edge, she played house with the worms he used as bait, off a fly rod, when bugs jittered on the water around her father's wadered thighs, at sundown, in curdled amber light. *Running into the sun* . . . she'd name them—the worms—for all the imaginary friends who gave her the kind of safe love she never could find in real life. One time, her father caught a baby turtle rather than a fish, and the girl cried until he proved to her that the turtle was still alive. *But I'm running behind* . . . and off the turtle went, upriver. Off the girl went, with her father. On the street, here she comes now. She's making her own way back.

Next, a lady in heels clips the girl's bashed up knee with her shoe's spike, then throws a buck on her lap. The pain to her knee gets the girl. She shoots up from the street, sharp like a needle. There's froth from her mouth all down her front and tangled up in the ends of her hair that's come out from under her hood. Her face is the same shade as a bloated Seattle sky that holds water like a fresh cadaver. The whole grey mess makes misshapen shadows across her face.

Lemon stumbles to standing. Hey, I don't need your fucking money, she slurs at the lady's backside walking away. Lemon wipes her mouth with the cuff of her sleeve. All around her she feels her father, the scent of English Leather. Had he been here? She crumples the lady's bill and stuffs it down the pocket of the jacket. Smells like home. Maybe he would know where to find his daughter? Her headphones are crooked, now covering only one ear. She looks like a beaten dog.

Obviously, you do, the woman says, spinning on her heels back toward her. She extends another bill. Lemon looks this one in the eyes. They're not turned down or sullen. No, it's not pity Lemon sees. This woman's wide eyes are hateful. She's angry, disgusted. Just take it, she says. Get off this street for a day. Go get yourself some coffee or something.

Lemon snatches the money from the lady's hand. Fuck you, she says. I mean, thank you, then bows like a court jester.

Better yet, get a *fucking* job, the lady says walking away, heels clicking against the street.

Her bottle's empty. Her Hero's up and vanished. She unzips the jacket, slides the headphones around her neck. Where did this shit come from? she wonders, then checks her pockets for what's left. Not even enough for a pint. Lemon craves for Whiskey like having another lover on the back burner. She loves the taste of it and its deep wooden color like maple syrup. She loves the way Whiskey enters her and turns her into an entirely different kind of lady—a proud lioness, all balls and brazen, and . . . visible. Fuck the world! Fuck it all, Whiskey roars, and the girl comes out of herself completely. Whiskey says, You are *not* transparent. You are *not* homeless, kid—these streets are yours. You *are* the world, Whiskey shouts. She likes to sing on Whiskey, fuck on Whiskey, fight on Whiskey. There's nothing Lemon would refuse to do high on Whiskey. Unless it required her to leave the bottle behind. That's why the two brawled today—Lemon and Space. When Space told her to, Find me some damn motherfucking money, Lem. I love you, baby, you know I do, but this shit's gonna get real *in your face* if you don't figure out how to make us some money, it doesn't take her more than two seconds to slap him right in the mouth. How dare you, Lemon says. I am not your slave, while Whiskey says, Go fuck yourself, under its breath.

The girl's lost all sense of time. And Space. Where the fuck is he? She makes her way to the 7-Eleven, pissed and sick. She's been running with Space since leaving Minneapolis on a Greyhound bus in the middle of the night on a ticket she'd bought with stolen cash from her father's wallet. Space had a handle of cheap whiskey he offered to share with her from two seats behind. Soon enough, he had shifted into position beside her. Lemon offered him Xanax from a bottle prescribed to her mother, and off they went, in and out of love and consciousness, by the time they hit the North Dakota state line.

Space measured his blackouts in distance. Twenty-six hundred miles, he told Lemon, all the way to West Virginia on a Grey-dog. Can you believe *that*? he said. I never was no good at sports growing up on the Tulalip Res but, drinking? He tipped his face toward her and whispered, Well drinking I can win at every time. When he arrived in West Virginia, Space said he'd had no clue whose idea it had been to go all that way. It didn't matter, he said. All he needed to know was that he loved her—the tourist cowgirl with long legs and blond hair he'd met late one night while working at the Res casino. And he did, he said, he *did* love her. Which, to Lemon, seemed plenty enough for him.

At the time, Space's ramblings during that ride seemed important, as if she should write the information in ink on the back of her hand. A cheat sheet for later to prove she really knew him. Like how his real name was Shelton. Mama named me after Chief William Shelton, can you believe *that*? he said. Only ever been the chief of two things in my whole dang life: drinking and making love. Space grabbed his crotch with one hand, took a swig off the bottle with the other. Turns out, his West Virginia woman named him Space, For what's between my ears, he said. Then he laughed. He only laughed that one time the whole ride with Lemon. The other thousand miles Space cried and cried and cried some more, one fat tear after the next, tumbling from eyes behind mirrored glasses that he never—not once— removed, even in the dark.

He cried about how after a year of bliss in the West Virginia countryside, his woman kicked him out of their trailer after finding him ass up with her younger cousin which, he explained, was completely unavoidable given how she came on to him like that. Like what? Space went on, With her bare titties spilling right out her shirt and onto my face! Almost poked my eye out and just like that—BAM!—there I was with them things in my mouth. She sure as hell knew better than to leave them two alone, he said, especially with a handle of Southern Comfort on a Sunday. Then he said, I will probably end up loving you, baby girl. But know right now, I am not built for fidelity. And there was this giant of a man—a staunch Snohomish with elegant sloping features in steel-tipped cowboy boots and a black bandana holding back his thick long hair—heartbroken, like a toddler in timeout.

She meant to keep going west, all the way to the northern border. She doubted her parents would go as far as Canada to find her. The night of Lemon's departure, her mother had insisted on dinner together, the three of them. Lem, come on down. I made meatloaf, your favorite, her mother shouted up to her. The last of her Heroin, barely enough to keep her well, had just been shot into a vein on her foot from a needle she stored in a tin box at the back of her underwear drawer. Lemon imagined her mother's hands kneading raw meat in a glass bowl, red flesh gunked between each knuckle. Murderer, her mother would be thinking about her daughter, as she scraped the meat from each finger. She'd chop onions, the sting of loss oozing from her burning eyes. Meatloaf for the murderer. She wondered if the small things reminded her mother most of what the surviving twin had done. How rotten she really was.

Vanishing twin syndrome. Third trimester. One girl flattened in the womb, then absorbed by the other. That's how her mother said the young intern described the condition as if forecasting the lives of both girls by the death of one. The Heroin made Lemon imagine the young doctor as excruciatingly handsome when he delivered the news, dressed up in a fancy suit like a TV weatherman would wear. Heroin, her Hero. He'd have a wide veneered smile, pointing here, gesturing there. Hero-in. He'd say, In Minneapolis tomorrow, expecting mother, Charlotte, will mourn a fetus papyraceus while the temperature rises to new heights in the Martin family home with the experience of excruciating turmoil. The heat will eventually come down, temporarily cooled by severe intoxication of all family members, but this is to be followed by massive floods of tears and rage, so don't make life plans just yet. Hero. That doctor along with her sister would take up residence in the crack-house of her muddied mind as if relentless squatters. Lucy, painted in abstract each time she closed her eyes, reduced to a piece of wilting fruit wrapped in a filmy skin like cellophane. But her Hero. Hero made *everything* better. Cartoonish and impermanent.

Not tonight, Mom. I'm not hungry.

Nonnegotiable, Lem. Come down, her mother said.

Lemon dragged herself to standing. Fuck, she said. The girl knew she was wearing her mother thin. Just last summer, her parents finagled a job for the girl working for Les Hamlin, an old family friend, who Lemon forever associated with forced hugs and bad breath. On family holidays, he'd pull her into him way too close and hold on, forcing her to squirm out from under his large arm. She'd be the counter clerk at his deli, Hamlin's Ham & Stuff. The marquee alone made the girl want to vomit. You need some structure, Lemon. The routine will be good for you, her mother said.

She made it through her first few shifts. Then, a week in, her Hero ran out on her, and she hadn't been paid yet. She knew exactly what to expect being forsaken by her Hero. At the register, when her bowels began to untangle, she doubled over, crippled, intestines knotted so tight they could haul a semi. Volts of pain from the nerves down her limbs made her legs throb then twitch like lit firecrackers. Withdrawal was a slow torture, like being skinned alive. She asked Mr. Hamlin for permission to use the restroom. In the stall, she hailed Mary, promised God, and negotiated with the devil, just to make it through the day. Better yet, kill me, just do me in, here and now. Reflected in the mirror, she saw a monster. Her wasted arms braced her body with bent elbows that looked like little wings. The girl stared into dark eyes like holes in the sunken canoe of her face. She splashed herself with cold water and returned to the register. Then, when Mr. Hamlin's back was turned, she dumped the tip jar into her apron and ran for the door. When she returned home later that night, Hero in hand, her mother was waiting for her after a phone call from Mr. Hamlin. Lemon wasn't shocked.

These are the times I wonder what would've happened if Lucy had made it. I am so *disappointed* in you, the mother said.

Of course you are, Mom. It's hard to be the perfect twin when the other twin is *dead*, the daughter said.

Before going down for their last dinner together, Lemon boxed her paraphernalia carefully and stuffed the tin toward the bottom of the one backpack she'd take on the road. Her father sat at the head of the table across from her mother. An empty seat, always the same, faced Lemon. She pushed meatloaf around her plate with a spoon, droopy eyes on the blank spot across the table that was supposed to be her sister. Her mother drank two glasses of red wine, sips against silence. Lemon's father went on to talk about his day as if trying to bury the absence in the room. Her mother drank more. The girl felt them watching her with suspicion like a trainer to an unfed tiger. She knew they were never sure of what she'd do. Lemon's stomach turned at pink grease on her plate. I'm done, she said. Then, she shoved back from the table, leaving her mangled meatloaf behind.

Later that night, she sat on the carpeted stairs leading to their second floor to eavesdrop on a discussion between them. Her father's voice was low and collected, rational. Her mother's words were slow and slurred. This sloppiness would make stealing the Xanax on Lemon's way out all the more reasonable. She was the louder of the two.

I found an empty bottle of booze underneath her bed, Rod. It's like she wanted me to find it, she said.

She's a teenager, Char. I mean come on. You're being dramatic.

She's nineteen, an adult. I can't do this anymore. I'm afraid for her. I think we need to consider getting her some help.

We've tried that already, her father said.

Of course they were afraid, Lemon thought. I'd be afraid of me, too.

Her mother's voice got softer then. Lemon crept down to the bottom stair to listen closer. I wonder about the two of them, her mother said. If Lucy would've been like this, too, had she made it out of my fucked up womb to see the light of day. Lemon's just not right, Rod.

The pills, Charlotte. Lemon could hear him shake the bottle at her. Just stop with these. You're not making sense. None of this is your fault. It's not your body's fault or Lemon's or mine. The girl needs us. We have got to pull things together, here. You're not setting a good example for her.

And *you* are?

Lemon stopped listening to them argue then. She tiptoed back upstairs to finish packing her bag considering how fitting, how truly tragic and ironic, the whole mess would become. She knows they'd think it was unnatural for her to leave without saying goodbye. In the end, it would all be right. She'd save them from the monster she was, help them salvage what remained between them as if refrigerating the leftovers of a perishing family. One twin, sweet, vanishes before birth. One twin, embittered, vanishes after. She shut the front door tightly behind her, careful to close it all the way. Then, she locked up and slid her key under the door for them to find later, after she was gone.

At the Seattle Greyhound stop, Space begged her to stay. Baby, please, look, you and me, we are like, what's that old movie? Bonnie and Clyde! You and me are like them. Then, he cried even more which absolutely disgusted her, coming down as hard as she was. When the bus left the Seattle terminal, Lemon watched its backside from a bench outside in the rain. Under a street lamp, rainbows reflected off oil on the ground. Pacific fog mixed with exhaust rising from under the bus as it pulled away, northbound at midnight. Lemon smoked while Space rested his head on her shoulder. She finished the Whiskey. Two things comforted Lemon most about the man twice her age: his desperation, and not having to look in his eyes. The rest, it was decided, she could deal with. Last she saw before her blackout was the butt of the bus and a child waving until the girl shrank into the size of a small baby doll, then disappeared around the road's next bend.

Now, she swears she'll strangle the life out of him if she ever sees Space again. Inside 7-Eleven, there's her favorite cashier, Kofi, distracted by the small TV behind the counter playing reruns of The Simpsons. At the counter, she slides a package of gummy bears into her pocket then asks, Kofi, you seen Space?

Lemon sunshine, you look good today, no? This show so funny. Kofi sucks on sunflower seeds, then spits each tiny shell into his hand. Swannies. Check there, he said.

Swannies. The one bar in Occidental Park that doubles her pour at lunchtime if she promises the bartender, Zeek, that she'll eat something. Jesuschrist, Lem, at least a fucking carrot stick or whatnot. App's on the house if it will keep you from what happened last time.

Last time? It was an *accident* for chrissakes. Plus, Johnny Boy's the one who told her what happened after the fact, and he's completely unreliable. A regular daytime drinker with a wife and a couple kids. He told her he'd been laid off from Boeing recently. Seems to Lemon he's spending his days hiding out at Swannies. One time, he tried to stick his tongue down her throat right there at the bar. All she remembers is Listerine beneath the booze on his breath and the prick of his mustache against her upper lip. She still ended up in the stall with him that day for a line of blow off the lid of the toilet seat. When she took his coat off, she remembers thinking he smelled like the oldest guy she'd ever been with by a mile.

What *had* happened last time? Johnny Boy told her that she'd seized right there in the middle of the bar. There she was, she'd been told later, like a real epileptic, foaming at the mouth, bashing her head against the floor, her hands crippled like claws. Zeek and Johnny, they swore to her they'd tried to help. And there was another guy there, too, Johnny Boy said. An old guy he'd seen around a few times. You know the one. Never drinks, just stares at a full glass. Yeah, that one, real calm like. He knelt beside her the whole time, cradling Lemon's head in his hands. His glasses slid down his nose, but he never let go, not once. When it was all over, the man placed her head on the floor like a jeweler sets a precious stone. Damn it, boy, he shouted at Zeek. Make yourself useful, and get me a wet rag. He smoothed the hair away from the girl's forehead, and laid the rag across. Then, like nothing had happened at all, he went back to his stool. It was creepy, Lem. Like he knew you or some shit, Johnny Boy said. Lemon came out of the episode good as new, but she'd bitten her tongue so for the rest of the week she lisped, her high voice sounding more like Mike Tyson than a white teenage girl with a Minnesota accent. She hasn't been back to Swannies since.

She opens the front door to the bar slowly. Zeek sees her first. Oh fuck, here we go, he says, wiping the bar down. It's too early for customers, just a few daytime drinkers straggled along the bar.

I'm just looking for Space, man. You seen him? Lemon starts walking toward pool tables at the back.

Have a seat, Lem. Zeek pats his hand on the bar. Free pour, he says.

She sits. He sets a glass down and there's her beloved, her manly man, Whiskey, right from the bottle, with grooves like ripped muscles, a torn label that reminds her of Zoro. Whiskey winks while Zeek pours long and tall. Suddenly, all the world's edges seem softer.

Lemon drinks from her glass as if making love. In Johnny Boy's seat to her right, an old man stares through a short glass filled to the rim. No ice.

You gonna drink that? Lemon asks.

Your boyfriend left with a girl who wasn't you out the back door just as you walked in.

What'd you say?

You heard what I said. He's gone. You're better off without him.

Lemon looks to Zeek. Zeek shrugs, then pours her another.

How do you know who my boyfriend is?

I've been watching you. Been coming around here for a while.

Lemon picks up her glass and moves over to the stool beside the man. What do you mean, you've been watching me? You some kind of perv, or something?

I'm too old to be perverted. Don't have the stamina for making trouble.

Well what then?

I saw you earlier today on the street. The jacket's a little big, but it ought to keep you warmer out there. The headphones are old. They're still good though. When I saw you, I thought you'd like to hear some music in your condition. My wife, April, used to stretch those very headphones across her belly when she was pregnant.

These are *yours*? She takes the headphones from around her neck and sets them on the bar in front of them. Then, she leans toward him. What is this, man? I'm not your project. You give me all your shit, like I belong to you. I'm not yours to fix, and I don't need your fucking charity.

Zeek walks over, lifts a bowl of nuts to run a rag down the bar. Come on, Lem. The guy's just trying to be nice, he says. This is the one that helped you out the last time you were here. Remember? He raises his eyebrows and sets the bowl down. Least you could do is be friendly. Zeek cocks his head toward the man.

That's what all perverts do, she says. They're all very *nice*. Lemon drinks thinking of old Lester Hamlin and his long hugs.

No, it's just that you remind me of my daughter, the man says. How she might have been, that is.

How's that?

Beautiful. Red hair. With a fire in you.

I'm a mess. Never have done one good thing in my life.

At least you're alive. You're here. That's something.

Lemon looks at this man. He seems to be withering with the time taken to pass each moment. She thinks he might be dying, right here, in front of her. Then, he removes his wallet from his back pocket. Inside is a photo behind a plastic slot. He pries out the photo and sets it on the bar. When he caresses it, Lemon notices the skin on his hands, loose and wrinkled, his knuckles gnarled like knots on driftwood.

You can't save me, Lemon says. No one can.

I can try, he says. You must let whoever loves you *try*.

She drinks. The man's glass remains full and untouched. Then, he begins. He tells her about April, his dear. How he'd met her in summer on Vashon Island at the Strawberry Festival. From across the street at the parade, he'd seen her for the first time through a pair of wooden legs as tie-died banjo players stomped by on stilts. He tells Lemon about that wild tangerine hair of hers. How he'd smiled quickly when their eyes met, pretending he didn't know she was looking at him. How he'd watch April in silhouette, against low light, outside their RV—looking in, under California moonlight, when they'd parked under the stars overnight on their trip to Sonoma, wine country. How in the capsule of the RV, when she lifted her nightgown, her naked body brought a wash of sweetness and earth over him, like plums and pine. How they'd make love and after, he'd prop himself on his bony elbow while she sat cross-legged, her books strewn about them. Then, she'd close her eyes and pick one out to read to him. Rumi and Neruda, lyrics from Laura Nyro or Joni Mitchell. He even told Lemon how his mother named him. That she'd said giving birth to him was like passing an ostrich through a keyhole, his long limbs and fingers, bony elbows and knees. *Not a soft spot on the boy*, she'd said. *That's why I named him Artist. To soften him up a bit.* And how when Art found April, his level, sensible mind curved. How she could coil his straightest angles. Art tells Lemon everything in one broad sweep. It's like he's ticking off an inventory and cleaning up what's left in back.

When he ends, his face is still straight ahead as if he's boxed in a confessional and Lemon's the priest. She can't find anything shameful about it. These are the things people remember about love, Lemon thinks. Then, suddenly, she remembers sitting on the knee of her own father. Him holding her tightly at the waist, bouncing her while he sang, *You are my sunshine, my only sunshine. You make me happy, when skies are grey.* Where's your daughter now? Lemon asks.

Art cups his hands around the full glass in front of him. He'd gotten too drunk the night of his daughter's birth, barely made it to the hospital in one piece. When he arrived, the baby was already crowning, and April was heaving her final push. When the daughter arrived, April softened completely, breaking open like a river rushing toward its falls. Art kissed his wife's head. But then, then, all was silent. There were no cries. The mother jolted toward the child. When April realized her baby girl was gone, she hardened solid, from a rushing river into ice frozen over. Her heart was shattered. The doctors had to pry the infant from her mother's stiff hands.

I haven't had a drink since, Art says. Not for thirty-one years. He runs his finger around the rim of his glass. When I found her in our bed a couple weeks back, I thought she was sleeping. Her cheeks were still pink, alive. We'd been married over half a century when she died. Now that she's gone, there's nothing much left to make up for. Art pulls the drink toward himself. He turns toward Lemon and looks in her eyes for the first time. Then he says, Making mistakes is not the same as being one. You are not a mistake, and you still have *time*.

Suddenly, from the back door, in comes Space. Hey, Lem, I been looking for you, baby. How you doing?

Lemon downs Art's drink and sets the empty glass down. She saunters over to Space as if Zoro himself. She slaps him, lightly, upside the head. Space brings his hand to his hair. He's got tears in his eyes. What the hell was that for? he says like a spanked child.

You know what that's for. I'm done with all this. And I hate when you cry. Then she turns to Art and says, It's not your fault, Art. It was never your fault.

Outside, she has to walk uphill, all the way to 1st and Pike to find a payphone. No cell, and hardly any cash left at all. She knows the phone number by heart.

Dad?

Lemon, is that you? Where have you *been*? My God, Lem, thank God, it's you.

Why'd you name me Lemon?

What? You know why, Lem. Where are you? Just come home. Or I will come get you. Tell me where you are.

Tell me, Dad.

You are my sunshine, my only sunshine, her father cries when he sings to her over the phone. *You make me happy when skies are grey.* His song trails off as she pulls the receiver away from her face and sets it down on the hook. She walks back down to Occidental Park where she sits on a park bench—that one—the one from a month or so ago. When she was loaded from the Heroin and drunk on boxed wine. She carved an anarchy symbol in tiny scratches on the metal of the bench's backrest. She sits back and imagines the very back row of the Greyhound bus, the last seat, looking ahead with rain hitting the windows behind her.

Susannah Sheffer's (she/her) chapbook This Kind of Knowing was published by Cooper Dillon Books in 2013, and her full-length collection Break and Enter was published by Kelsay Books in 2021. Her poems have appeared in The Threepenny Review, Copper Nickel, Tar River Poetry, Poet Lore, and other journals. She is a clinical mental health counselor who frequently works with people who have experienced trauma, and her book Fighting for Their Lives: Inside the Experience of Capital Defense Attorneys was published by Vanderbilt University Press in 2013. She lives in Western Massachusetts.

The Apple
Susannah Sheffer

The truth is I wanted them
to choose me. Disobedience, yes,
but maybe something else: fealty
to the complication of their own
bodies, the problem
of curiosity: taste and see, taste and
find out. Before, I mattered only as much
as everything else. Now
I mattered more. They made me
myself and they made me part of them,
and in this new disturbance
we were ripe and full of our
desire to know what came next.

Kris Faatz *(rhymes with skates, she/her) is a Baltimore-area pianist and writer. Her short fiction has appeared or is forthcoming in Streetlight Magazine, Black Fox Literary Magazine, Baltimore Review, and other journals, and has received recognition in various contests, most recently winning Tiferet Journal's 2020 fiction competition. Her first novel, <u>To Love A Stranger</u> (Blue Moon Publishers, 2017), was a finalist for the Schaffner Press Music in Literature Award. Her second novel, <u>Fourteen Stones</u>, is forthcoming in 2022 from The Patchwork Raven (Wellington, NZ). Kris teaches creative writing independently and with the Community College of Baltimore County.*

Tejedora
Kris Faatz

For Lee

The quilt held all of the child's favorite things. His mother was a gifted tejedora, weaver: she had the rare knowledge that let her spin the stories and songs themselves, the pictures and scents and tastes, into the yarn that she worked with her clicking needles. The human mind was fragile. Memories could slip through the cracks too easily, but the child would never lose those pieces of his past as long as he kept the quilt close.

The child chose the yarn for each new, palm-sized square. Sky-blue for the clapping game he played with his best friend. Cinnamon-brown for the taste of horchata, the sweet drink made with milk and rice and vanilla. Sunlight yellow for the hugs his abuela gave him. His mother knitted the squares and pieced them together into a mosaic as singular as the boy himself. From the time when he was old enough to choose the colors, the child knew how much the quilt mattered. Each time his mother knitted a new square, he felt the yarn curling through his thoughts, winding around the things he loved to hold them tight and safe.

The mother used her knitting needles to create her magic, or what other people would call magic, but she kept something else close to her: six spiders, each about the size of a walnut, carved out of wood. They were beautiful, made by her grandfather for her grandmother, who was also a tejedora. Their sleek bodies and slender legs were veined with the grain of the pine. Their eyes, made out of polished glass, glittered like dewdrops in the sun. The mother kept the spiders near her but did not use them yet. For anyone else, they would only have been beautiful carvings. For her, when her hands grew too stiff to work her needles anymore, the spiders would—as they had done for her grandmother—do what spiders did best.

The mother often had trouble getting new colors of yarn. There on the poorest edge of Tegucigalpa, where rival gangs tore at each other with knives and gunfire, the simplest things became luxuries, and luxuries were as remote as heaven. The mother braved the dangerous streets day after day, to get to the better neighborhoods where beautiful things could be had for the asking. She didn't ask for anything for herself, only the colors she wove for her boy.

Someday, she knew they would have to leave. She could scrape some kind of life for herself here on the edges, but she wouldn't lose her son to the drug gangs that had taken his father or let him grow up in a place where tomorrow was barely a hope. She had a sister away to the north in the Estados Unidos. If she and her boy were lucky, if God did care for the weak, they might make it that far.

She didn't know what might happen on that journey across land she couldn't imagine. As the time came when she knew they would have to go, she did something she had never done before.

Her son had never asked her to weave herself into his quilt. Mamá was always there, as certain as the patched roof of their shabby house and the faded paint-peeling walls. During their last handful of nights at home, as May burned into June, the mother chose her own favorite colors. Rose, gold, and the pale green of new grass. Carefully, she wove them into the mosaic, making a border around her child's memories. She did it in case, sometime soon, he would need the memory of her arms holding him.

#

Estevan tried as hard as he could to like his Tía Aurelia and Tío James. They had come and gotten him out of that place in Texas where the American soldados, the soldiers in their dark-green uniforms and thick boots, put him and Mamá. Mamá had said she and Estevan would be safe once they got across the river, but the soldados caught them at a place called El Paso and put them in a building with thick concrete walls and bars on the windows. Then one day they came and…but Estevan tried not to think about that. He had nightmares about it every time he slept.

Tía Aurelia was Mamá's sister. She told Estevan she was a little younger than Mamá, but she said that when she was seven years old, the age Estevan was now, people had thought she and his mother were twins. She called him *Este*, the way Mamá did, and *mi amor* and *mi cielo*, and she told him she was so glad to finally meet him, she'd always wanted to meet her sister's boy. She told him she had missed Mamá so much when she married Tío James and moved to los Estados Unidos. She had never stopped worrying about the family she had left behind in Tegucigalpa. She said she knew everything was going to be all right now, the American soldiers would let Mamá go soon, and Mamá would come to Arizona and be with her family.

Estevan tried to like his aunt, but she didn't look anything like Mamá. She didn't have the silvery hair or the crinkly lines at the corners of her eyes and mouth. She didn't have the quick hands that made wooden knitting needles click like crickets chirping at night. She didn't have thick knitter's calluses on her thumbs and fingertips. Tía Aurelia couldn't knit at all. And she didn't know how to make the foods Mamá loved to cook, even though her huge kitchen was smooth and shiny and clean, and she had more food in her tall refrigerator than Estevan thought anybody could ever eat. He had never been in a place like the apartment where his aunt and uncle lived. Everything looked and smelled brand-new, the carpets and paint and the wooden furniture.

Tía Aurelia smiled and told him how well-behaved and grown-up he was, and said he shouldn't worry, he should relax and feel right at home. But this wasn't his home, this place where everything tasted and sounded wrong. His aunt and uncle talked together in English and Estevan didn't understand. Every night, he woke up out of dreams that made him feel like he was drowning.

He didn't tell his aunt and uncle about the dreams. He also didn't tell them how he counted every single day since he'd lost Mamá. Then, on the night of the twenty-first day, he woke up screaming.

The little room in Texas had bars on its one little window. The American soldier-woman came in with a gun like the ones the bad boys carried back home. She caught Estevan by the wrist, she was pulling him out of the little room, he didn't know where she was going to take him. Mamá sat on the wooden bench, under the little window with the bars on it. She cried and twisted her hands in her lap and her face looked like soft dough with holes for eyes. And Estevan yelled for help as loud as he could. He fought and kicked at the soldier-woman's heavy boots, but she hung onto his wrist and dragged him to the door and he couldn't get his arm loose. And Mamá sat there on the bench crying and didn't get up or reach for him or say one word.

Estevan heard himself screaming out loud. *No! I won't go! Mamá, help!* The darkness in the bedroom clutched at him and his heart bang-bang-banged in his ears. He fought his way loose of the tangled bedsheets. His quilt, the quilt Mamá made him, had fallen on the floor. He heard footsteps coming fast down the hall.

Tía Aurelia turned the bedroom light on. The glare hurt his eyes. "Hijito mío," she said. She sat on the bed and touched Estevan's face with her soft hand. Mamá used to smell like yeast bread and cinnamon, but Tía Aurelia smelled too sweet, like the lilies they had in church. "You had a bad dream?" she said.

Estevan nodded. He didn't like her calling him a little boy, and he didn't want to remember the soldier-woman in her big boots. If he stayed very still and quiet inside himself, maybe everything else would go away.

Tía Aurelia picked his quilt up off the floor. "Here. This will help." She wrapped it around his shoulders as if he was a baby. "Your mamá made it for you, I know," she said. "You were dreaming about her, weren't you."

Estevan nodded again. His throat hurt so much he couldn't talk anyway. The quilt felt warm around him. He remembered the clicking of Mamá's knitting needles, how she'd told him he would always remember the most important things, as long as he had his quilt with him. But he didn't want to think about those things, because then he might cry.

Tía Aurelia said, "I remember how much your mamá loved to knit. There never was anybody else as good as her, from the time we were little." She looked close into his face and smiled. "Your grandmama tried to teach me too, but I never could learn."

She said it as if she was telling him a joke. Estevan couldn't smile. She went on, "Your grandmama was so proud that Luci was a real tejedora. You know what that means, don't you?"

Anger bubbled in Estevan's stomach. His whole life, he'd known about Mamá's magic with the yarn and the needles. He probably knew more about that magic than anybody, especially Tía Aurelia who couldn't even knit. But when his mouth opened, he heard himself say, "Mamá's name is Lucera."

Tía Aurelia looked surprised. "Of course, mi amor. But when we were little, everybody called her Luci. I was Lia." She reached out to touch the quilt, the sunshine-yellow square near Estevan's hand. "So did she pick out this color, or did you?"

She was making him talk. Estevan wanted to yank the quilt away from her, but it was safer to sit very still. "I picked it," he said.

"What did your mama put in it?"

Estevan swallowed. His eyes felt like he had gotten dirt in them. "Abuelita," he said. "When Abuelita gives me a hug."

Tía Aurelia's eyes looked sad. "I haven't seen your grandmama in a long time," she said. "I remember her hugs." She touched the sky-blue square on Estevan's shoulder. "What about this one?"

"My best friend." Estevan didn't have to touch the square to hear the song he and Alejo sang or feel their hands clapping against each other. When he and Mamá got ready to leave their old house, she'd told him he might not be able to see Alejo anymore, but he didn't need to be sad because he would always have the quilt to remember with.

Now his aunt had hold of the edge of the quilt. "And this green is Luci's favorite color," she said. "Or one of them anyway." She ran her thumb back and forth along the yarn. "When she had her quinceañera, she wanted a dress this exact green, and she wanted a bouquet of pink and yellow roses. Your grandpapa said it cost too much, but your grandmama said, a girl only has her fifteenth birthday once."

Estevan didn't want to hear about that, or think about what Mamá had said, that last day in their old house before they left. He could hear the words in his head anyway.

"I don't want you to be scared, but it won't be easy to get where we're going. If anything happens, if you and I end up in different places sometime, everything will be all right as long as you keep your quilt with you. You'll do that, won't you?"

He had never seen her look so serious. He'd felt scared, even though she said not to, and he didn't know what she meant about *different places*, but he tried to sit up straight and show her he knew how to be a man.

Now it didn't matter how still he sat on the bed, or how still he tried to stay inside himself. He was ready to cry, but Tía Aurelia was still sitting there holding onto the quilt as if Mamá had made it for her and not him.

She said something very quietly in English. He caught the name "Luci." Anger made his face hot. "What did you say?" he demanded.

For a second, she looked at him as if she thought maybe she shouldn't answer. Then in Spanish she explained, "I told your mamá that she was smart to put herself in your quilt."

Estevan stuck his jaw out and clenched his teeth so hard they hurt. He was *not* going to cry. But Mamá put herself in his quilt. She thought sometimes they might end up in different places…and she sat there on that bench and cried when the American soldier-woman took him away. She didn't make the woman stop. Now he was here, and she was still there in the little room with the bars on the windows, and it had been twenty-one days.

Tía Aurelia touched his face again. "Hijito, I know it's hard. You miss her so much. But it's going to be all right. We're going to help her get out of that place, and then she'll come here, and we'll all be together."

Estevan didn't believe it. Not when Mamá had let the soldier-woman take him.

He didn't want his aunt's hand on his cheek or her sad, worried eyes, or the bright light in the room or the quilt wrapped around him. He jerked away from her, yanked the quilt off, and threw it on the floor again. Then he burrowed under the smooth sheet and pulled it over his head to shut out the light.

"Go away," he said. Mamá would scold him for talking so disrespectfully, but she wasn't here.

For a long minute, nothing happened. Then the bed moved as his aunt got up. She touched his shoulder. "Mi amor," she said, "don't you want your quilt back?"

Everything will be all right as long as you keep your quilt with you.
But it would never be all right again.
"No," he said. "I don't."

He lay perfectly still until the light went out and he heard her footsteps going away.

#

Lucera knew how lucky she was that Aurelia and James had been able to take Estevan. Every day she offered prayers of thanks that she had a sister in this country, with a husband who was an American citizen, and that the two of them had responded at once when the American soldados had taken Lucera's boy away from her. She knew where Estevan was and that he was safe. For this, she must give thanks for the rest of her life.

She didn't know what was going to happen to her. The American soldados had her in a prison in the city called El Paso, in Texas. They said she was a criminal for trying to come into the country. She knew the word asylum, but the soldados didn't want to hear it. The Spanish-speaking American lawyer who tried to help Lucera had told her that she might stay in jail for many months before anyone would listen to her reasons for coming here. Even if they did finally hear what she had to say, they might decide to send her back to Honduras. Estevan, now in the care of an American citizen, would stay behind. Lucera told herself she would manage alone. As long as she knew where her son was and that he was growing up healthy.

Every hour of every day, while she sat on the cot in her cell, or sat in the big room with the other women and ate the tasteless food she was given, Lucera tried to remember how lucky she was. Too many other mothers didn't know where their children were. She and the other women weren't supposed to talk together much, but the guards didn't really stop them. Lucera had met three women, two from Mexico and a fellow hondureña, whose children had also been taken somewhere else. The four of them helped each other stumble from one day to the next.

Jimena, one of the Mexican women, told Lucera and the others that she'd wanted to fight the soldier who took her toddler from her. "I'd have put my fist through his jaw," she said, one morning during Lucera's third week in the jail, scooping bland breakfast cereal on her spoon. "But if he fired his gun in that tiny room, the bullet could have gone anywhere." Lucera pictured the bullet ricocheting off the cement walls, the way the gang boys' bullets had chipped sidewalks and gouged houses back home. Jimena said, "My baby and I didn't come all this way for some pendejo's gun to tear her belly open." Lucera saw that too, and wished she didn't: the tiny body so violated, the blood running free. Jimena laid her spoon on her tray with a solid *clink*. "But," she said, "you can bet your life that nobody is going to keep my girl from me."

She had the most hope of the four of them. Lucera admired her restless strength, like a tiger in a cage. Inés, the other hondureña, was more like Lucera herself, small and soft-voiced. She answered Jimena, "I don't know. The lawyer says we can't do much."

The words clawed Lucera's heart. Jimena's jaw set. "American lawyers. What do they know?"

The other mexicana, Pilar, touched the place at her throat where Lucera knew she must have worn a crucifix or saint's medal before the guards took all of those things away. Pilar was the oldest of the four of them. Her husband and two teenage boys had ended up in other prisons somewhere else. "Mother Mary will help our children," she said. "I don't ask for help for myself."

Neither do I. Lucera didn't answer out loud. She liked these women—they had to like each other, keep each other alive—but she never said much when they were all together. She couldn't tell them she was a tejedora. In the prison, of course, that meant nothing: the guards had taken her needles, along with the six priceless spiders her grandfather had carved against his wife's old age. Still, she had given her child a gift that the other mothers could not. Even if Este never saw her again, he would not forget her.

She couldn't tell these grieving women that. Worse, she couldn't tell them what she herself had done when the American soldado took her boy away. Every hour of every day, even as she tried to give thanks to God for the mercies He had granted her, she heard her son's voice, screaming.

No! I won't go! Mamá, help!

She and Este had come so far. When they crossed the river at El Paso, the last of her strength seemed to rush out of her, but she had thought they were safe. Then the soldier came to take Este away, and in the face of that horror, Lucera had nothing left to give. She had felt the tears running down her cheeks as her son reached out for her, shouting and fighting the soldier with all his strength. Even her hands had been too heavy to lift.

Then Este was gone. She had not even managed to tell him she loved him.

"Lucera." Jimena's voice reached her from across the table. "Mujer, are you going to drink that juice or what?"

Lucera realized she was staring at the plastic cup on her tray. "I'm not thirsty," she said. "Do you want it?"

Pilar was the one who answered. "No, Luci, you should drink it. You don't eat enough as it is."

"Look out, Luci," Jimena said. "Pilar's adopting you."

The other women laughed. The sound made Lucera feel dizzy, like a rush of fresh air. *Luci*: only her sister and mother called her that. She drank the too-sweet juice, which had no real oranges in it that she could taste.

If only she knew exactly what the place looked like where Este spent his days. She had only gotten to talk to Aurelia twice so far, and the guards only gave her a few minutes each time. On the phone, she and Aurelia had both cried and tried to pretend they weren't crying, and they had both talked about how the minute the americanos realized they had to let Lucera go, Lia and James would buy her a plane ticket to fly to Phoenix to be with her family. They had pretended to have answers for everything. As much as Lucera's whole soul ached to hear her son's voice, in real life instead of memory and imagination, she had let the minutes run out while Lia was still on the phone. She told herself it was because it would be hard and strange for Este to talk to her while she was still in this place. It would upset him too much. She tried not to admit, even to herself, that she didn't want to know if he had given up on his mother.

He still had the quilt. Any time he wanted, he would be able to feel her arms around him. Sitting in the big cell, with the other women's voices murmuring around her, Lucera tried to hope.

#

The morning after the bad night, twenty-two days after he lost Mamá, Estevan woke up with something heavy and cold in his stomach. His face felt stiff, as if it would hurt to blink his eyes. He felt the way he sometimes felt when he had to be sick, except he felt empty too, as if something that belonged inside him had gotten out and snuck away during the night.

It was early. The sun had just gotten up. Back home, Mamá would be awake already, but Tía Aurelia and Tío James slept later. Tío James worked in an office where they didn't need him to come in until after nine. Tía Aurelia didn't go to work. Soon she would get up and make Estevan a bowl of the thick warm cereal she said was good for him, and she would watch to make sure he ate enough of it. It was all right if he put some milk and sugar on it, but otherwise it tasted like warm nothing. This morning he didn't think he could open his mouth to put anything in. Even if he could, he didn't think it would fit in his stomach, with that cold heavy thing inside.

The quilt lay on the floor where he had thrown it last night. He looked at it over the side of the bed. The cold thing in his stomach seemed to get bigger, but the rest of him felt emptier than ever.

Everything will be all right as long as you keep your quilt with you.

The soldado with her gun. Mamá sitting there with the tears running down her face. Estevan couldn't forget things. The quilt wouldn't let him.

When he pushed the sheet back and got out of bed, his whole body felt so cold he got chills, but he picked up the quilt and held it away from him the way you hold smelly trash. Some of it still dragged on the ground. Carrying it that way, he tiptoed out of his room and down the hall.

Tía Aurelia kept scissors in the kitchen, in the drawer next to the stove. She used them to cut up meat. They were very sharp. Estevan wasn't supposed to touch them, but he knew how to be careful.

He took them out, touching them only by the handles. He put the quilt on the table and picked up the corner square, the one that was bright yellow for his abuela.

The scissors went *snick,* clipping through the stitches Mamá had knitted. Estevan watched the yellow square falling on the table in little pieces, the loose ends of yarn working free like worms. At first he felt nothing at all: just quiet. And then…

Abuelita kneeling in the yellow sunlight. Estevan was so small that the tiny yard looked huge, Abuelita so far away. His legs felt wobbly and he was scared he would fall, but he took one step forward. Abuelita called to him —"come here, little one, that's it"—and he took another step and another. Then her warm hands reached out and caught him, and she swooped him up into the sunlight, and he was laughing…

Estevan cut faster. The cold thing in his stomach slid around like ice melting in a cup. He cut bigger pieces, slashing the scissors through the middle of one square and then another. The colors tumbled onto the table and floor.

Alejo came up the road shouting. "Este, come on! Mamá says we can play till supper!" Estevan ran outside into a summer afternoon where the blue sky reached down to touch the cracked pavement, and the air tasted like being happy…

…In the kitchen, Mamá opened a glass bottle full of creamy white milk. "Hijito mio, it's time to make horchata." Estevan's favorite drink, that Mamá only made for special days because the milk and vanilla cost a lot, but today was his fifth birthday. He could already taste the sweet rice and feel the smooth liquid sliding down his throat. Nothing ever tasted better…

Now the cold thing inside him was gone. Estevan's stomach felt full like a huge ball of water, and he was going to be sick, he was going to cry. The scissors went faster and faster, the sharp blades moving *snicksnicksnick.*

…rain on the roof in the old house, rain on the roof in winter, but inside it was warm and dry and safe. Mamá was baking bread. Her eyes didn't look tired; she was humming a song…

…last Christmas when Estevan and Alejo searched every street and gutter for empty bottles and old nails and bits of broken wood. They took everything they found to the junk shop and got money for it, and Estevan took his share to Abuelita and together they got Mamá a shawl made out of soft fabric the color of roses. The way her eyes looked when she opened the package…

He was crying now, the tears running hot down his cheeks and dripping off his chin, and he couldn't stop to wipe them because he had to keep cutting, he had to, he had gone through almost the whole quilt now…

Mamá's voice singing to him. Mamá's arms holding him. The smells of cinnamon and yeast bread. Mamá.

Estevan heard someone sobbing, an awful sound like an animal hurting. The scissors were still moving but his hand didn't want to open and close them anymore. There was still a little bit of quilt left, with some of the gold and pink and green stitching.

Then somebody was calling out, "Este, no! What are you doing?"

Somebody's hand wrapped around his. Estevan tried and tried to keep the scissors moving, but somebody tugged the scissors away, tugged the last of the quilt out of his other hand, and he wanted to struggle and kick and yell for help, but he couldn't breathe and everything hurt so much. Then somebody knelt down, somebody wrapped their arms around him, and Estevan caught a flowery smell and then his arms went around her too, his empty hands hanging onto the smooth fabric of her nightdress. The two of them held onto each other and they cried and cried, with the pieces of the quilt scattered on the floor all around them.

#

Lucera woke up knowing what had happened. Estevan had destroyed the quilt.

She had to know it because the quilt held a piece of herself. She felt it, the same way she thought she would surely feel it if her boy died, even if he was on the other side of the world.

At breakfast with the other women, she sat silent. Pilar tried to get her to have a spoonful or two of cereal, but Lucera shook her head and pushed the bowl away. Jimena asked her what was wrong. When Lucera didn't answer, the mexicana got angry.

"Mujer. You can't just give up." Jimena scooped up her own cereal and chewed it fast and hard, as if she could eat for herself and Lucera both. "You have to keep trying. Your boy needs you."

He doesn't want me. Lucera couldn't open her mouth to say the words. If only she had given Estevan the carved spiders, if she had thought to do that before the guards took everything. But there hadn't been time, and then they had taken him too. She wasn't living through anything worse than what these other mothers suffered, but for the first time, she could not offer the prayers of thanks she knew she must.

Early that afternoon, Aurelia called the prison. Lucera didn't especially want to talk to her, but then, nothing seemed to matter much. Her body felt light and empty enough to blow away on a breeze.

"Luci." Lia's voice on the other end of the phone sounded startlingly clear, as if she was standing there in the room with the grimy beige walls instead of her mysterious apartment in Phoenix. "Luci, you have to tell me how to fix it."

Lia couldn't do any such thing. She had never known how to knit. Even if she did, she could not recapture Estevan's memories and put them back where they belonged. She was not a tejedora. For all the good it had done, Lucera knew she herself might as well not have been either.

"Luci," Lia repeated. If she was upset, Lucera couldn't hear it. Her voice sounded firm and determined. "Tell me what to do."

Lucera knew she didn't have much time on the phone. It would be so easy to stand here silent until the few minutes ran out.

"Hermana," Lia said. "Sister. You should have heard him crying. He cried himself out. He misses you so much."

Lucera found she could speak. Her voice sounded as if she had swallowed a mouthful of dust. "He wants me?"

"Wants you?" Now Lucera heard her sister's tears. "Luci, we picked up every scrap of that quilt. Every little piece of yarn. We put them all in a grocery bag. He held onto that bag and he wouldn't let go of it, not to wash his face or eat or anything, until I told him his mamá would tell us how to put it all back together." Her voice sounded clear and steady again as she said, "I promised him you would, Luci. You've got to."

Lucera felt as if she had spent the past weeks, ever since the soldados had taken her son, buried underground in the dark. Now a tiny shaft of light broke through. "Is he there, Lia? Can you put him on the phone?"

"Yes."

The minutes were draining away too fast now. There was a way, if only Lucera could keep her thoughts together. She couldn't knit the quilt back together herself, and Lia couldn't do it, but those were Este's memories, and he knew how it felt when they wove together with the yarn.

"Mamá?"

At the sound of his voice, Lucera's heart scrambled up her throat. For a moment she felt so dizzy she thought she would faint.

"Mamá, I'm sorry. I cut it up. I was so mad…"

He was crying, her baby. She ached to reach through the phone line, across the distance she couldn't measure, and take him in her arms. Her voice had to reach out instead. "Este, precioso, it's all right. I think we can fix it, but I need your help."

She heard him gulp. "I don't know how to knit."

If she could teach him, someday. If she could hold him again. Could God allow her such miracles?

"It's all right," she said again. "I'll tell you what you need to do. Listen closely, now."

"Yes, Mamá."

She told him. So much of it depended on what he knew about the weaving, and the fact that the memories were his. As Lucera explained what he needed to make, and what to do with it once he had it, she found herself praying again, offering thanks and asking God's help to see this through.

When she finished, Este was quiet for a moment. Then he said, "I can do it. But what if they're not very good?"

The guard by the phone looked at Lucera meaningfully. Her minutes were almost up. "Don't worry about that, hijito," she said. "As long as you know what they're for, they should do the job."

"I'll do it," he promised. Then, "Can I talk to you again next time?"

The next time Lia called her. Lucera wanted to tell him that, soon, they wouldn't have to talk on the phone, that she would be free and they wouldn't have to be apart anymore. "Yes, you can," she said. "We'll talk again before you know it."

She had to hang up now. Before she did, she told him what she hadn't managed to say that day in the cell.

"I love you, hijito. You know that, right?"

"I love you too, Mamá."

Lucera waited for the click on his end of the line before she hung up the phone. The dingy room was full of light.

#

Estevan didn't tell Mamá on the phone, or Tía Aurelia either once he hung up, but he didn't see how it was going to work to do what Mamá said. But he would do it, because she was really there in that place in El Paso. He'd heard her voice on the phone, so he knew.

He and Tía Aurelia went shopping to get what they needed. The store had things like fabric and needles and yarn, and paints and special paper to draw on. The air was cool and smelled like dried flowers. Estevan sniffed it and looked up at his aunt. "Mamá would like it here."

"She would," Tía Aurelia agreed.

She didn't say *we'll bring her here*, or anything like that. After this morning, after the quilt, she didn't tell him everything was going to be all right, or Mamá would come be with them soon, or those other things she'd said before. Estevan knew that Mamá was in trouble, and maybe they wouldn't be able to help her get out of it. That was the truth. But he'd heard her voice on the phone, so that was true too. And maybe they really could fix the quilt.

They found an aisle that had boxes of modeling clay stacked on a shelf. You could get a box with different-colored sticks of clay in it. And when they found another aisle that had pipecleaners, all different sizes and colors, he laughed at the big thick ones that were covered in glitter. Tía Aurelia laughed too. "I don't think we should get those, do you?" she said.

"No." Estevan thought about what it would look like, if he made what Mamá had told him to make, with those thick glittery pipecleaners. He wondered if maybe, if they could put the quilt back together, he could put in how it felt to laugh so he wouldn't forget again.

They chose some thin black pipecleaners, and finally, a thin black marker that would draw on the clay once it dried. Back home, Tía Aurelia set everything out on the kitchen table.

"Do you want to be by yourself to do this?" she asked.

Estevan studied her. Maybe, after all, she did look a little bit like Mamá. It was something about the way she looked at him. "Can you help?"

"Of course."

Estevan picked the colors of clay and rolled out balls of it like Mamá had said, six bigger ones and six smaller ones. He tried to make them very neat. Mamá said that didn't matter, but he thought if they looked good, they might do a better job. He put them in pairs, one small one with one big one, and pushed them together so they would stick. Tía Aurelia cut the black pipecleaners into pieces, all the same length. Six sets of eight pieces. She helped him bend the pipecleaners and push them into the clay, as evenly as they could.

It didn't take very long. After the clay dried, they drew two little black dots at the front of each small clay ball. Then they stood back and looked at what they had made.

Six spiders sat in a row on the table and looked back at them. Two were blue, two were green, and two were yellow. Mamá had told Estevan to pick his favorite colors. She said that was very important. They were too big to be real spiders, and they were made of clay, and they had pipecleaner legs and eyes made of marker ink…but somehow, even though they didn't look real at all, Estevan wouldn't have been surprised to see them start scuttling around on the table.

Tía Aurelia thought so too. Looking at them, she smiled and shook her head. "I don't like spiders, mi amor. Let's put them where they belong."

The grocery bag of quilt pieces sat on Estevan's pillow. He put the spiders inside it carefully, one at a time, and tied the bag's plastic handles together to shut it tight.

He didn't know if it would work. He remembered Mamá's wooden spiders that her own abuela had given her, and how she'd told him that she would use them when she got very old and couldn't knit anymore. But they had been beautiful. His spiders were made out of modeling clay, with pipecleaner legs. Could they really do what she said?

He had to try. As he slipped the bag under his bed where nothing would bother it, the way Mamá had said to do, for just a second he caught the scents of bread and cinnamon.

#

The quilt held all of the child's favorite things. Most of all, maybe, it held his mother too, some piece of her breath and thought and life. When the mother woke up in the prison and felt as though torn pieces of her heart had been knitted back together, she knew her boy had made the magic work.

Lying on the narrow cot, looking up at the bars on the cell windows, she imagined the spiders her son had made. They would not have been elegant like the carved ones she had lost, but he had made them with his hands and love. She imagined them there in the plastic bag that held the scraps of his quilt, rushing back and forth on their pipecleaner legs. They had done what spiders did best.

The quilt could not be exactly the same as it was before. Her heart, and her boy's heart, could not be what they had been before the prison and the soldiers. Not even if a miracle happened and the two of them found each other again, and she had no way of knowing if that could ever be.

But now, and always, he would have all of his favorite memories, kept safe where he would never lose them. Whenever he wanted, he could feel her arms holding him tight.

Kathleen Stancik *(she/her) is a Northwest poet whose work has appeared in Cirque, Windfall, WA129 Digital Chapbook, Twenty-Fourth, Shrub-Steppe Poetry Journal, Take a Stand:Art Against Hate, and others. She was a featured poet at the Inland Poetry Prowl in 2017 and was awarded the Tom Pier Prize by the Yakima Coffeehouse Poets in 2018. She presented at Writing Against Constraints in Ellensburg WA, in June, 2021.*

A Blessing of Oranges
Kathleen Stancik

In the end what they remembered were the oranges
how he'd watch Saturday Night Fights
on the black and white TV while they sat close
around the frayed card table

praying for a pinochle
his wife's hair wrapped in pin curls
tied with a head hanky
ready for work at four the next morning.

They remembered the moans when his man lost
how he'd get up slow from
the ottoman he'd pulled close to the screen
disappear to the kitchen and

return with oranges still in their jackets
cut carefully into eighths
always eighths
the scent of oils anointing the room.

He'd watch them pull
the flesh with their teeth
discard spent skin into bowls
droplets of juice blessing their fingers.

He'd chuckle, content,
then return to the ottoman
lean forward for the next fight
elbows on knees
chin at rest on his palms.

Despy Boutris's *writing has been published or is forthcoming in Copper Nickel, Ploughshares, Crazyhorse, AGNI, American Poetry Review, The Gettysburg Review, Colorado Review, and elsewhere. Currently, she serves as Editor-in-Chief of The West Review.*

Out of the Ether

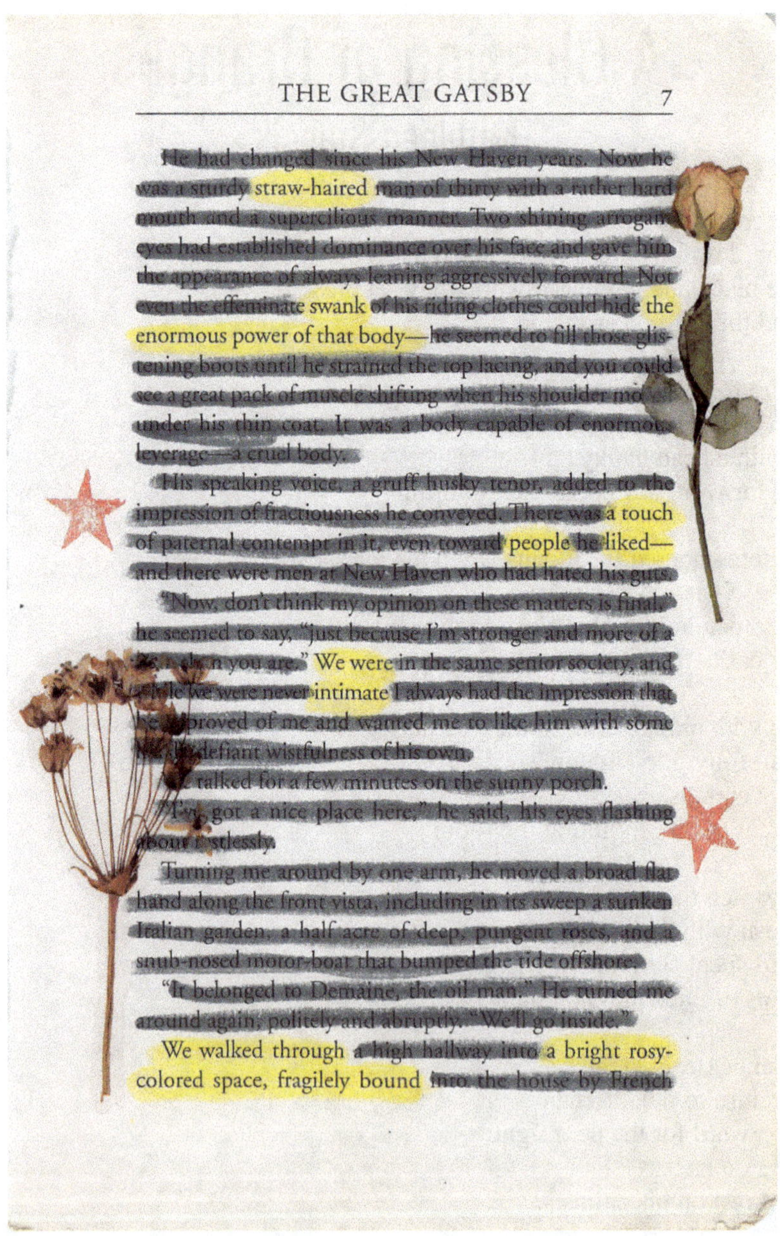

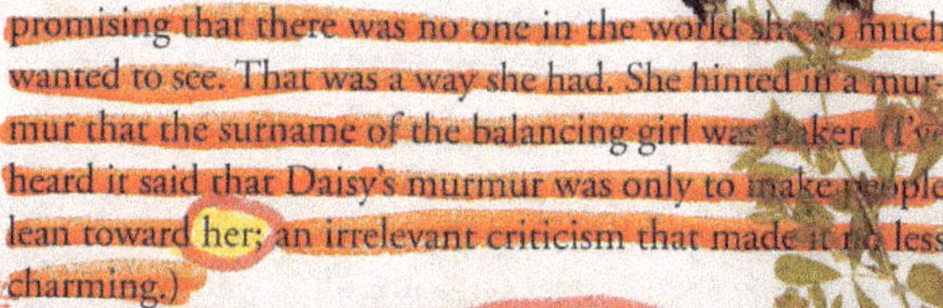

promising that there was no one in the world she so much wanted to see. That was a way she had. She hinted in a murmur that the surname of the balancing girl was Baker. (I've heard it said that Daisy's murmur was only to make people lean toward her; an irrelevant criticism that made it no less charming.)

At any rate, Miss Baker's lips fluttered, she nodded at me almost imperceptibly, and then quickly tipped her head back again—the object she was balancing had obviously tottered a little and given her something of a fright. Again a sort of apology arose to my lips. Almost any exhibition of complete self-sufficiency draws a stunned tribute from me.

I looked back at my cousin, who began to ask me questions in her low, thrilling voice. It was the kind of voice that the ear follows up and down, as if each speech is an arrangement of notes that will never be played again. Her face was sad and lovely with bright things in it, bright eyes and a bright passionate mouth, but there was an excitement in her voice that men who had cared for her found difficult to forget: a singing compulsion, a whispered "Listen," a promise that she had done gay, exciting things just a while since and that there were gay, exciting things hovering in the next hour.

I told her how I had stopped off in Chicago for a day on my way East, and how a dozen people had sent their love through me.

"Do they miss me?" she cried ecstatically.

"The whole town is desolate. All the cars have the left rear wheel painted black as a mourning wreath, and there's a persistent wail all night along the north shore."

"How gorgeous! Let's go back, Tom. To-morrow!" Then she added irrelevantly: "You ought to see the baby."

"I'd like to."

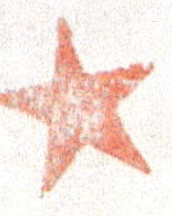

I looked at Miss Baker, wondering what it was she "got done." I enjoyed looking at her. She was a slender, small-breasted girl, with an erect carriage, which she accentuated by throwing her body backward at the shoulders like a young cadet. Her gray sun-strained eyes looked back at me with polite reciprocal curiosity out of a wan, charming, discontented face. It occurred to me now that I had seen her, or a picture of her, somewhere before.

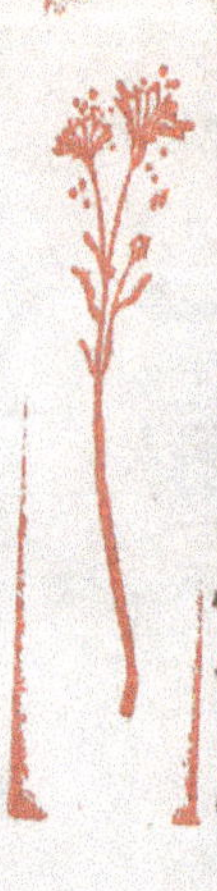

"You live in West Egg," she remarked contemptuously. "I know somebody there."

"I don't know a single——"

"You must know Gatsby."

"Gatsby?" demanded Daisy. "What Gatsby?"

Before I could reply that he was my neighbor dinner was announced; wedging his tense arm imperatively under mine, Tom Buchanan compelled me from the room as though he were moving a checker to another square.

Slenderly, languidly, their hands set lightly on their hips, the two young women preceded us out onto a rosy-colored porch, open toward the sunset, where four candles flickered on the table in the diminished wind.

"Why *candles*?" objected Daisy, frowning. She snapped them out with her fingers. "In two weeks it'll be the longest day in the year." She looked at us all radiantly. "Do you always watch for the longest day of the year and then miss it? I always watch for the longest day in the year and then miss it."

"We ought to plan something," yawned Miss Baker, sitting down at the table as if she were getting into bed.

"All right," said Daisy. "What'll we plan?" She turned to me helplessly: "What do people plan?"

Before I could answer her eyes fastened with an awed expression on her little finger.

"Yes. Things went from bad to worse, until finally he had to give up his position."

For a moment the last sunshine fell with romantic affection upon her glowing face; her voice compelled me forward breathlessly as I listened—then the glow faded, each light deserting her with lingering regret, like children leaving a pleasant street at dusk.

The butler came back and murmured something close to Tom's ear, whereupon Tom frowned, pushed back his chair, and without a word went inside. As if his absence quickened something within her, Daisy leaned forward again, her voice glowing and singing.

"I love to see you at my table, Nick. You remind me of a—of a rose, an absolute rose. Doesn't he?" She turned to Miss Baker for confirmation: "An absolute rose?"

This was untrue. I am not even faintly like a rose. She was only extemporizing, but a stirring warmth flowed from her, as if her heart was trying to come out to you concealed in one of those breathless, thrilling words. Then suddenly she threw her napkin on the table and excused herself and went into the house.

Miss Baker and I exchanged a short glance consciously devoid of meaning. I was about to speak when she sat up alertly and said "Sh!" in a warning voice. A subdued impassioned murmur was audible in the room beyond, and Miss Baker leaned forward unashamed, trying to hear. The murmur trembled on the verge of coherence, sank down, mounted excitedly, and then ceased altogether.

"This Mr. Gatsby you spoke of is my neighbor——" I said.

"Don't talk. I want to hear what happens."

"Is something happening?" I inquired innocently.

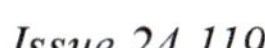

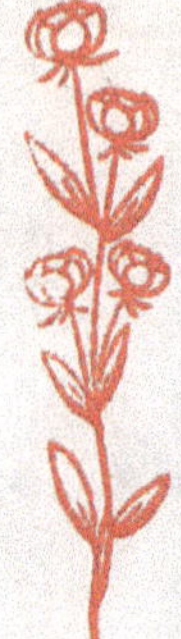

"You mean to say you don't know?" said Miss Baker, honestly surprised. "I thought everybody knew."

"I don't."

"Why——" she said hesitantly, "Tom's got some woman in New York."

"Got some woman?" I repeated blankly.

Miss Baker nodded.

"She might have the decency not to telephone him at dinner time. Don't you think?"

Almost before I had grasped her meaning there was the flutter of a dress and the crunch of leather boots, and Tom and Daisy were back at the table.

"It couldn't be helped!" cried Daisy with tense gayety.

She sat down, glanced searchingly at Miss Baker and then at me, and continued: "I looked outdoors for a minute, and it's very romantic outdoors. There's a bird on the lawn that I think must be a nightingale come over on the Cunard or White Star Line. He's singing away——" Her voice sang: "It's romantic, isn't it, Tom?"

"Very romantic," he said, and then miserably to me: "If it's light enough after dinner, I want to take you down to the stables."

The telephone rang inside, startlingly, and as Daisy shook her head decisively at Tom the subject of the stables, in fact all subjects, vanished into air. Among the broken fragments of the last five minutes at table I remember the candles being lit again, pointlessly, and I was conscious of wanting to look squarely at every one, and yet to avoid all eyes. I couldn't guess what Daisy and Tom were thinking, but I doubt if even Miss Baker, who seemed to have mastered a certain hardy scepticism, was able wholly to put this fifth guest's shrill metal-

where. I woke up out of the ether with an utterly abandoned feeling, and asked the nurse right away if it was a boy or a girl. She told me it was a girl, and so I turned my head away and wept. 'All right,' I said, 'I'm glad it's a girl. And I hope she'll be a fool—that's the best thing a girl can be in this world, a beautiful little fool.'

"You see I think everything's terrible anyhow," she went on in a convinced way. "Everybody thinks so—the most advanced people. And I *know*. I've been everywhere and seen everything and done everything." Her eyes flashed around her in a defiant way, rather like Tom's, and she laughed with thrilling scorn. "Sophisticated—God, I'm sophisticated!"

The instant her voice broke off ceasing to compel my attention, my belief, I felt the basic insincerity of what she had said. It made me uneasy, as though the whole evening had been a trick of some sort to exact a contributary emotion from me. I waited, and sure enough, in a moment she looked at me with an absolute smirk on her lovely face, as if she had asserted her membership in a rather distinguished secret society to which she and Tom belonged.

Inside, the crimson room bloomed with light. Tom and Miss Baker sat at either end of the long couch and she read aloud to him from *The Saturday Evening Post*—the words, murmurous and uninflected, running together in a soothing tune. The lamp-light, bright on his boots and dull on the autumn-leaf yellow of her hair, glinted along the paper as she turned a page with a flutter of slender muscles in her arms.

When we came in she held us silent for a moment with a lifted hand.

Jeff William Acosta (he/him) is a Filipino poet from Ilocos Sur, Philippines. His poems have been published in 聲韻詩刊 *Voice & Verse Poetry Magazine, The Dark Horse, CAROUSEL, Matter Press, Prairie Fire and elsewhere.*

Silentium
Jeff William Acosta

Light sets each sequined body
       of saltwater before they fold

into themselves again and again
against each wave—the sea's

sadness, I recognize
       grief when I see it. That summer,

I submerged my body. Unearthed
the sands sitting on the blades of my shoulders.
On my spine I filter salt
       from silt like cleansing, like baptism.

That if my voice arrives, it may sound ceremonial
       cacophony of cawing crows
subtly scattered in the wake
of what I, even the dead, could not hear.

(I guess) I am still alive—that I know, for a reason
better not knowing:
       what I found is a resemblance of my brothers
being pulled, their tongues, away

from their mouth. Shrapnel
between the eyes—a small collateral

damage. On the ocean's edge, I plunged,
headfirst,
       to assemble segments
of what seemed to be a part of me, almost,

and I wouldn't mind if it's a figure
of my own death. Isn't that love? *Yes,*

I know.
I kept watching.

(forgive me) I kept watching behind me
in fear—I couldn't help it

because fear has its own language
of worship and grief provides a living
remedy—my nepenthe. My body

is hollow, hyacinth against riptides as I try
to be real in this world where it cost too much

> *to wake up,*
> *to speak*
> *even at this time of peace*
>
> *when I am supposed to hear you*
> *I do not hear you*
>
> *even though my eyes are wide, wide open*

I can only hear clutch clicks
        of cock-backed pistols—pressed
names on our throats to relive
        echoes of ghost hymns,

like humming, like relearning the word for crippled
air after rains—earthly, like rust, like wounds

but briefly, against waves, these lips
against a face

not mine
until it's faithfully sealed.

Leslie Stonebraker *(she/her) been published in The Kenyon Review and Entropy. She is working on a collection of short essays about miscarriage, pregnancy, and parenting. In her day job, she leads a research team for five Broadway theaters. Leslie lives in New Hampshire with her husband and two rambunctious kiddos. She is an MFA candidate in creative nonfiction at Vermont College of Fine Arts.*

Knock Knock
Leslie Stonebraker

More often than this, surely.

I haven't felt him since this morning, when I woke to pain strumming down my right calf that only dissipated when I rocked slowly from my heels to my toes. Gently, gently.

I think he kicked then. Softly, softly. Or did he? Now my belly feels different: lighter, hollower. Or does it? I don't remember what it felt like yesterday.

I sensed him once around lunchtime, deep inside my pelvis, a tentative knock, knock.

As the late afternoon sun slants across my desk, my consciousness searches for evidence of fetal activity while my brain searches the Internet for answers.

Amazon raises her hand first, offering a $69.99 fetal Doppler to monitor the baby's heartbeat from the comfort of my home. But none of the palm-sized devices rate more than two stars.

Google rebukes sister Amazon, warning, "This is a prescription device that should only be used by a medical professional."

I think about calling a medical professional, and then I think about driving all the way to the OBGYN office just to hear the baby's heartbeat, and then I think I'm being silly.

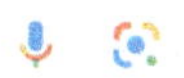

It's too soon to be worried about kick counts—ten movements an hour is standard in the third trimester, but I'm still several weeks away. I know fetuses sleep 90-95% of the time, mostly during daylight hours when they're rockabye lulled by parental movements. I know there's probably nothing wrong with the baby inside my bump.

That doesn't stop me from worrying.

I am not a very good embryo incubator. I'm surly and stressed and sore. Worse, I'm borderline negligent, eating far too much chocolate and not nearly enough dark leafy greens. Still, I need to know he's all right, and movement is my only ready measure of fetal health. I prepare a warm brownie with a scoop of melty ice cream. An umbilical influx of sugar should wake him, gently, gently.

He doesn't budge. Not even when I follow up with a short glass of orange juice and a tall glass of icy water.

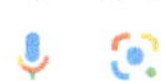

"Jiggle the belly," Google replies. I try jiggling the belly. The hard spot that might be his head doesn't shift. "Do jumping jacks," Google suggests, so I jump once, my breasts crashing onto my chest in a slap of pain. "Lie down," Google promises, so I lie on the couch and wait and wait and wait until I have to get up to join a video call for work. Nothing.

"It's ok, hun, just relax," my husband texts when I tell him I don't feel right. "Give it time. Deep breath."

He knows why I'm fearful, the reason I carefully monitor my expanding body and the reason I try not to. He was there three years ago when the bleeding wouldn't stop, when I miscarried my first pregnancy, when we learned, too late, that surgery could have corrected the anatomical abnormalities that caused it. He held me afterward as the tears fell, softly, softly.

Today I try not to cry. I get distracted by work—forgetting to pay attention to the baby, forgetting to worry—and then I worry about not worrying. Is he okay in there? Only the nurse licensed to wield the prescription fetal Doppler monitor would know, and now it's well past office hours.

I am a fetus's landlord, and I don't treat the building well. My Fitbit barely registers 2,800 steps a day, mostly logging trips to the kitchen for snacks. Raising the 30 pounds of my two-year-old to sit on the shelf of my baby bump barely counts as weightlifting. I already admitted the lack of leafy greens, but let me now confess the two bowls of Cinnamon Toast Crunch I ate last night. Okay, it was three bowls. And I didn't even have the excuse of trying to get the baby to move at the time.

Suddenly, I remember waking on my back this morning. Did I unwittingly choke off the baby's blood supply by sleeping that way?

Unlikely.

Still, I check my underwear for blood. Check for blood again. Check how far along the pregnancy app thinks I am. Check the limit of viability.

Fifty percent chance of survival for a birth at 24 weeks. I imagine discovering this baby had died—from the sugar, from the lack of activity, from the back sleeping, from any of a thousand reasons that would add up to it being my fault again. I imagine delivering him stillborn. Imagine asking the nurse for an epidural, already being in enough emotional pain. Imagine watching dark monitors that should have been alive with activity, imagine pushing for each pointless count of ten, imagine his body tearing through mine, imagine his beginning being his end.

Imagine looking at his little face. Stroking his tiny hands. This time, saying goodbye.

And then, predictably, at night, while I chase the oblivion of sleep, finally he wakes, this stubborn wonderful boy of mine. Slams me hard in the gut, tap dances on my bladder. A sequence of knocks against my insides like fingernails on lacquered wood.

I breathe a small laugh of wonder. Gently, softly, I knock back.

Soon Jones *(none/she/they) is a half-Korean, full-lesbian writer and failed missionary from the rural countryside of the American South. Their work has been published in Moon City Review and Emerge: Lambda Literary Fellows Anthology, and can be found at www.soonjones.com.*

Downburst

Soon Jones

In the morning darkness on my sister Ava Kim's birthday, I drive seven hours across state lines to my childhood home nestled in the countryside of Kentucky. When I pull up the gravel driveway shortly after noon, I'm the only one there.

Across the narrow, two-lane rural road are hundreds of sunken holes where there was once a forest, a few white clouds hanging mournfully over its grave. A man named Henderson bought up all the land around here after I left for college, dreams of a country suburbia dancing in his head. Soon houses will spring up like weeds.

My parents have already sold the field and moved back to the city about thirty miles away, and my half-brother Caleb got what was left. I should have fought harder for the farm, but I didn't.

Dust motes eddy around me in the old barn. I pick through my father's water stained tools, and take a shovel with good heft and a sharp blade.

Two trees separate our backyard from the field, which have grown so close together their branches twist and mesh. The two-by-four swing my parents hung between them is still here, but the wood's rotted through and it likely won't survive another storm.

I take a few steps past the trees and try to recall something I dreamed when I was a child. I wander deeper until the green ocean swallows me up.

I start digging where it feels right. The soil is dark and rich as cake, full of worms and centipedes and other slithering creatures. The shovel pierces through earth as easy as a knife through yielding flesh.

#

I turned seven on a Wednesday. When the presents had been opened, the cake eaten, and the other farmers had taken their children home, I sat by myself on the swing, looking out over my ocean, holding the new pocketknife Papa gave me in my hands. I caressed the pearlescent handle, traced the edge of the blade, both repulsed and excited by the possibility of being cut.

Caleb came up behind me and grabbed me by my shoulders, then yanked me backwards off the swing. My head hit the ground and the taste of iron exploded in my mouth and nose.

He took the knife away from me and said, "Knives are for boys. Here, I'll trade you."

He threw a spatula at my face, and the humiliation hurt worse. Then he laughed and walked away.

After dinner, we crowded in the living room to watch a movie. Ma was in the kitchen making more popcorn when Papa brought out one last present.

"Elise, why don't you come over here with that fancy new knife of yours and help me open this," he said, grinning wide.

Caleb glared at me from behind our father's head, and my tongue was thick and dry, swelling behind my teeth. This was the choice I hated most growing up: whose bruises would I rather bear?

"I lost it," I said.

Papa's smile faltered.

"What do you mean, you lost it?"

"I was out playing in the field and I dropped it. I can't find it."

Papa jumped up from the couch and grabbed my arm, yanking me up off the floor.

"You what?" he yelled.

Ma came running, yelling, "Franklin! Let go of her!"

Papa spun me around and spanked me with his bare hand, not even waiting to take me to my room first. Ava jumped up from the loveseat and clubbed him in the ear with her fist.

"Get your fucking hands off my sister!"

He slapped her across the face so hard her silver locket spun around her neck. Ma grabbed his arm and drew him back, and Caleb burst out laughing as they screamed at each other.

Papa had never hit Ava before. Because she was my mother's daughter, and not his, he was not allowed to punish her just as my mother was not allowed to punish his son. Either parent could hurt me, though, because I belonged to both of them.

Ava glared at Caleb, her face red and contorted, her nostrils flaring. She had never been afraid of him like me, and she had always been smarter. Quick as a rattlesnake, she pulled my knife out of his back pocket and threw it at my father's chest. Caleb stopped laughing as Papa bent down to pick it up off the carpet.

Ava banged through the back door. I chased after her into the fields.

"Ava! Come back!"

"Go back to the house, Elise," she yelled over her shoulder.

"You can't leave me with him!" I pleaded.

Ava came to me then and ruffled my hair.

"I just need a walk to cool down, okay? I'll be back soon," she said, and then left me adrift.

When I went back, Caleb's screams were echoing in our yard and Ma was smoking a cigarette on the back porch. It was the first and last time I ever saw her smoke. I sat beside her, and we watched Ava disappear into the far reaches of the field, dipping beneath the horizon.

"I'm sorry about your birthday," Ma said, and then she laughed bitterly. "I left the city to get away from violence, not have it localized to my living room. If I'd known this was the way they did things in the country, I never would've left."

She smoothed my hair down on my scalp. Caleb stopped screaming. Somewhere in the house, Papa slammed a door. I fell asleep on Ma's shoulder, where I could smell her strawberry shampoo.

I woke up in my own bed with Papa sitting on the edge. He put the last present beside me, placing my knife on top.

"That's okay," I said. "I don't want it anymore."

Papa nodded and took them back into his hands. He stopped in the doorway, silhouetted by the yellow hall light, and said, "I love you, sweet pea."

I had a nightmare that night. There were monsters in the field, swaying and grunting together, and the sound of iron striking soft earth. I knew in the dream-sense way of knowing that if I went too close to my window, one of the monsters would drag me through the glass and do terrible things to me.

And then I was in a park chatting with a woman selling ice cream. She floated in the air with black and red balloons tied around her waist, and she looked like my sister, but older and sadder, and then she floated away from me.

In the morning after, Papa was on the phone saying things like, "I know how teenagers are" and "I won't be angry, I just want to know," and my mother was crying on the couch.

I sat down at the kitchen table and Caleb took out two bowls, pouring us both cereal and milk. His right eye was puffy and there was a cut on his neck, peeking above the ribbed collar of his shirt.

"Where's Ava?" I asked.

He shook his head slowly and sat down across from me.

"Ava never came back last night."

Papa hung up the phone and went into the living room. Caleb and I didn't even touch our spoons as we eavesdropped.

"What did the Collins say?" Ma asked.

"Their boy Tom said Ava went to see him last night. She told him they should run away together, but he didn't think she was serious. Tom claims she went home after a while," Papa said.

"And the police?"

"They said they'd send a trooper out here tomorrow if she doesn't return by then."

Ma started crying again, and Papa shh-shh'd her.

"Don't touch me! You did this! You and your fucking son!" she snapped.

Caleb clenched his jaw and glared into his bowl. I stared at his nails.

"I'm going to make this right. I'm going to get in the truck, and I'm going to go looking for her. The Collins are already on their way. I'm going to make this right," he said again.

Papa left, and Ma stayed by the phone all day, jumping every time it rang. I went into the field and imagined finding Ava. She would be lying on the ground, and she would smile and tell me she was proud of me for being the only one smart enough to search the field. Then I would disappear into that green ocean with her.

Caleb walked out into the field after me, and even though I could hear him coming, I still jumped when he touched my shoulder.

"What are you doing out here, 'Lise?" he asked.

"I'm looking for Ava."

"You're in shock," he said, turning me back towards the house. "You go back inside with your Ma, all right? I'm going to take the four-wheeler and help Papa look for your sister. It'll be all right."

I let him walk me back to the house. I kept staring at his hands, at the dirt beneath his nails, the specks of dark brown smashed into his cuticles.

#

Clouds cover the sky like a thick film, and the wind is picking up. I'm sweating now, so I roll up my jeans and toss away my plaid shirt. My hair is plastered to my face with sweat. The muscles in my arms are burning, and my palms are raw.

The hole is up to my hips, then my chest. It's wide enough now you could hide a tractor inside. All I can see is dirt and the waves of grass above me, vibrant green against the dark gray of the sky. My body aches; I'm hungry and I'm thirsty. I should fill this hole and drive to a hotel before Caleb gets off work. I should forget about childish dreams.

The shovel strikes bone.

I drop on all fours and paw at the earth like an animal until I have a femur, cracked by my shovel, a tibia, some metatarsals, a spinal cord. A skull with a hole in the left parietal bone, fractures running down like rivers.

A necklace is tangled in the rib cage. My nails bend back when I try to open the locket. It's rusted shut, but patches of silver still shine, and on the back is a stylized *AK*.

I wrap the necklace around my fist, and my fist around the shovel. With my other hand, I twine my fingers around grass and roots and pull myself out of the hole, digging my toes and the blade of the shovel into the dirt to lift me up as the first drops of rain fall.

When I stand to my full height I see his truck first, parked half in the yard, half in the field, the driver's door wide open, the engine left idling. Then I see Caleb running towards me, parting the grass behind him, framed by the two trees in the distance. He's calling my name. He's making promises to explain himself. He's begging me not to tell our father.

The sight of him makes my lips curl. He still has that stupid fucking wispy blond mustache that he's been trying to grow out since last Thanksgiving. He once towered above me, but now he seems so small.

My blood boils and froths like waves smashing against the rocks. I grip the shovel tight with both hands and the wood bites into my palms. I shake with the promise of violence and whip the blade up over my head as my brother comes to me. Caleb's eyes are as wide as a fatted calf's standing before the butcher. I imagine Ava in the roiling storm clouds above us, and I wait for her signal. A torrent of rain suddenly crashes onto the remains of our farm.

And then, the thunder.

Karen Luke Jackson (she/her), *author of <u>GRIT</u> and <u>The View Ever Changing</u> and co-editor of <u>The Story Mandala: Finding Wholeness in a Divided World,</u> draws upon contemplative practices, nature, and family stories for inspiration. A poet, educator, and retreat leader with the Center for Courage & Renewal, Karen resides in a cottage on a goat pasture in Flat Rock, North Carolina. There she writes and companions people on their spiritual journeys.*

Lockdown
Karen Luke Jackson

Friday morning, fall of '64, the phone jangles.
I stop shaving, grab the black receiver.
No one's seen Gladys or the children for days.
I thank the caller, drive sixty miles to pound
on my sister's door. She edges it open, spirits me inside,
clicks the bolt. *Did soldiers follow you?"* she asks.

I scan the scene: a bug-eyed teen and an eight-year-old
frozen in their chairs. Carving knives line kitchen counters.
Sheets blacken windows. The weekend looming,
no judge in town, no possibility of commitment papers.
I ask neighbors to harbor the children,
take Gladys home with me.

My sister creeps into the house, sweater hooding head,
grabs my wife's arm and drags her through all six rooms,
searching closets, under beds, closing blinds.
She even climbs a footstool to check light fixtures
for bugs before declaring the house on lockdown.

All night, Gladys spins stories about disciples
fleeing Jesus' arrest, how after the crucifixion
his followers hid in an upstairs room. *They killed him
you know. I saw it! I was there."*

Fueled by black coffee and nothing else,
she paces the hall, hovers over our infant son
certain guards will kidnap the child if she fails
her vigil. I too keep watch beside the crib.
There she discloses her secret: *"You think I'm your sister,
but I'm really Mary Magdalene."*

The next morning, at the kitchen table,
I glance over my sister's shoulder, watch my wife crush
a white tablet, stir it into a mug of fresh brewed Folger's,
walk over and offer the cup.
Gladys lifts it like the chalice from which Jesus drank,
takes a sip then spits hot liquid in my face.
Someone here is trying to poison me.
I cringe as if Judas.

Monday morning, Judge Hendrix orders hospitalization.
A new hiding place, I assure Mary,
and kiss her cheek as deputies reach for her arm.

The Chair

Children and half-lit men
hurl baseballs to unhinge the chair
I sit in at the county fair,
a dollar a throw to raise money
for the women's shelter,

but in my dream or memory—
I cannot say which—the chair
where I'm strapped is a ducking stool
reserved for gossips, scolds who backtalk
husbands, and women like me who gather
herbs, mix potions and midwife babies.

I could not save the minister's wife
or the child. He cried *Witch*, claimed
I invoked the evil eye.
Sentence was swift.

When they hit the bull's-eye
I splash into a tank,
surface sputtering
everyone laughing

Each dunk prompts cheers
from a jeering crowd.
Plunge after plunge after plunge.

Kim Horner *(she/her) is the author of* <u>Probably Someday Cancer: Genetic Risk and Preventative Mastectomy</u> *(The University of North Texas Press, 2019). Her work has appeared in The Dallas Morning News, Seventeen, Minnow Literary Magazine, 805, and Parhelion. She is pursuing an MFA in creative writing from the University of Arkansas at Monticello.*

Robert
Kim Horner

I was typing frantically on deadline one afternoon when the phone rang. It was Robert. Everyone in the newsroom knew Robert Ceccarelli, a gruff guy in his fifties with a New Jersey accent, who frequently called with story tips. Sometimes he would call me or the news desk several times a day. Other times, we wouldn't hear from him for weeks.

I had less than two hours to file my story that day. Reluctantly, I picked up the phone. It was hard to have a quick conversation with Robert, who sometimes talked so fast his words became a blur. "Hey Robert, sorry. I'm on deadline so I can't talk long. What's going on?"

"I'm gonna to steal something so I can go to jail."

"Seriously?"

"I can't stay at the shelter no more."

He sounded more agitated than usual.

"What happened?"

Robert hated shelters. Some made you pay. Some made you pray. Most made guests leave first thing in the morning, forcing them to carry all their worldly possessions with them until the shelter reopened in the evening. One made men shower together in a large bathroom with no privacy. Any drug or alcohol use, no matter how slight, could put you back on the streets.

"I'd rather go to jail," he said.

There was no point in referring him anywhere else. Robert knew the system better than I did. I didn't know what to say. After a few minutes, I told him I needed to let him go so I could finish my story.

"I'm sorry, Robert. Please let me know what happens."

A week went by and Robert hadn't called. He didn't have a phone, so I couldn't call him. Whenever I didn't hear from him, I checked the Dallas County jail log first. I typed his name in the online form. There he was, close-cropped hair, stubble, with an angry expression in his mugshot.

Race: White. Sex: Male. Charge: Theft of property under $1,500—two priors. Bond Amount: $5,000.

Robert was a man of his word.

Later, he told me he had gone to Target and walked out with steaks and pork chops. Despite his best efforts to get caught stealing, the alarm didn't go off when he left the store. So, he went back in, shoplifted goods in hand, walked up to the checkout lane and told the cashier, "I'm going to steal this shit."

After speaking to Robert on the phone a few times, I finally met him in 2008 when I started following him for a year-long project for *The Dallas Morning News,* with the goal of examining the struggles of chronically homeless people to get off the streets. The federal government considers people to be chronically homeless if they have been on the streets long-term and have a disabling condition such as serious, persistent mental illnesses and/or chemical dependencies. People experiencing chronic homelessness often got blamed for their struggles, and even those who worked with homeless populations labeled people who were chronically homeless as "service resistant." However, Robert and most of the people I interviewed had not resisted help—they had tried all the services. Some had used the services so often they were called "frequent fliers." Were people experiencing chronic homelessness really failing the system, or was the system failing them?

I became interested in homelessness in college in the late 1980s when I read news coverage about people with schizophrenia, bipolar disorder and other illnesses being left to fend for themselves on the streets. At the time I felt like I was losing control of my own mental health. One day I was walking on campus with a friend when my insides felt wavy. I stopped. I was shaking, my heart was racing and I thought I was going to faint. "Are you OK?" my friend asked. "Yeah," I lied. Soon after that, I went to the student health center. A doctor there gave me Prozac and told me to keep taking it, even after my anxiety got worse and turned me into a crying mess. I stopped taking the medication and swore I'd never take another antidepressant.

My project on chronic homelessness was the kind of journalism I had dreamed of doing for years. I had received a Rosalynn Carter Fellowship for Mental Health Journalism to support my work, and I had a deadline and a sense of urgency. My newspaper and others across the country had been laying off reporters for years as the industry struggled with falling advertising revenue as people increasingly turned to other sources for news. It was a game of musical chairs, and after eighteen years in the profession I didn't know how much time I had left. Sooner or later, I'd be out.

Robert was an ideal source. He wasn't shy about being interviewed and photographed. He was starkly honest about his struggles. He signed releases allowing me to gain access to his medical records and put me on his jail visitor lists. And he checked in regularly, even with collect calls from jail. A tall former college football player, Robert didn't fit the stereotype of someone experiencing chronic homelessness. He had a master's degree and had taught special education when he lived in New Jersey. He said things started to fall apart when he tried crack cocaine, which a woman offered him at a nightclub. He said he never imagined how potent the drug could be. Once he came down from his first high, the depression was too much. "You need more," he said. Eventually, he said he lost his job, then his apartment, until everything he had was gone. Robert, an only child, left New Jersey after his mother died. He spent time in various states before heading to Los Angeles' Skid Row and then coming to Texas about twenty years before. Off and on he worked odd jobs, such as telemarketing, or traded food stamps to pay for drugs. Withdrawal often led to suicidal depression, which led to hospitalizations.

Watching people go through hospitalizations for depression forced me to face an illness I had spent most of my life trying to pretend I didn't have. I convinced myself that the hopelessness, crying, insomnia I often experienced was PMS, or that I just needed more exercise, or to change my diet, anything but accept that I had a mental illness. It would get better. It would get worse, until I would go to the doctor, desperate enough to try another medication.

One day, Robert called me from one of the most expensive shelters in town—the downtown hospital.

"I faked chest pains," Robert told me when he called.

Robert invited me to visit. There he was, wearing a gown, lying on clean, white sheets on a hospital bed, in a private room, resting in comfort. He spoke very quietly, not wanting anyone to hear the truth about why he was there. I watched Robert play patient as a nurse came in to take his vital signs. Then again, maybe Robert really did belong in the hospital at the time. After all, he desperately needed help. After a while I left, hoping he'd at least get a hot meal before being discharged back onto the streets.

New research at the time showed that the chronically homeless made up ten percent of the overall homeless population and used ninety percent of the services. I tried to determine how much taxpayer money had been spent on Robert, who estimated he had been in and out of drug treatment fifteen times. The public mental health system estimated it had spent more than $30,862 on Robert's care over five years. A two-week stint at Terrell State Hospital, the region's psychiatric facility, cost $5,222, and six months in the Dallas County Jail cost more than $8,000. Robert had been in and out of jail, prison, shelters, psychiatric facilities, rehabs, and housing programs for ten years and always ended up back on the streets. He estimated that he had been through rehab fifteen times.

"It's like a revolving door," he said.

The federal government was using the research to make what some called the "business case" for ending chronic homelessness. The idea was that the existing system was a waste of taxpayer funds since people would get treatment and end up back on the streets. The solution, proponents said, was to provide housing first, then add mental health and chemical dependency treatment services.

Robert desperately wanted to get out of the revolving door. He wanted to work as a tax preparer and continue to advocate for better services to help the homeless. In addition to calling the newspaper, Robert contacted local TV stations, spoke at city council, county commissioner and school board meetings, and to anyone who would listen.

"I know I can make a positive difference, to myself and other people."

Robert's experiences demonstrated exactly what was wrong with a system of chutes and ladders. For example, after one of his jail stints, Robert entered a promising housing program. But not long after, he called the newsroom, saying he had been kicked out.

"What happened?"

"I started using again."

He said drugs were easily available in the neighborhood where he was staying.

"It's all around you," he said. "It's a hell of a temptation. You meet a person you know from the streets, and your brain waves change right away."

Relapses, even though they are considered part of the recovery process, often send a person back to square one.

"I've been kicked out of a lot of places because I've gotten a dirty UA (urine analysis)," Robert said. "It makes it a lot harder because you got to scramble to find a new place."

Rehab programs routinely discharge vulnerable people right back to the streets, where it's difficult, if not impossible, to take care of basic needs, much less stay clean and attend outpatient treatment. People with illnesses that cause disorganized thinking are expected to remember follow-up appointments and navigate bus systems to get to clinics while living in shelters or on the streets.

Watching Robert and others experience chronic homelessness taught me that their struggles had less to do with a lack of willpower and more to do with a lack of adequate treatment. I know first-hand that, even with insurance, getting good treatment is much more difficult than it might sound. In addition, science is increasingly showing that chemical dependency is a medical, not a moral, problem. Yet people addicted to drugs are treated like criminals, not patients.

I doubt anyone was harder on Robert than himself.

"It's killing me," Robert said one time over the phone. "It's taking me all the way down. I'm getting desperate."

He compared addiction to a gnat.

"You try to push it away, but it keeps coming back. It makes you feel like a piece of crap. You get mad at yourself and feel like you're worthless."

Besides worrying about the end of my journalism career, and feeling overwhelmed at times by the pain, loss, and trauma I was witnessing, a year after meeting Robert, in January 2009, I discovered that I had a BRCA2 mutation, an inherited genetic variance that put me at an extremely high risk of developing breast cancer. I was forty-one—the same age my grandmother was when she died of breast cancer—and suddenly I was worried that I would not get to see my son, a toddler, grow up. It was time to go back to a doctor. I started a new antidepressant and, to my surprise, it worked. Therapy and a higher dose of medication finally helped me exit my own revolving door.

My series of articles about Robert and others experiencing chronic homelessness ran throughout 2009. The series won several journalism awards and was credited with helping gain rare state funding to address chronic homelessness, making it the highlight of my career. A couple years later, when yet another round of newsroom layoffs approached, I survived another round of cuts. However, I was reassigned to a different beat covering a suburban school district. I had dedicated years to covering social services, which included homelessness, housing, and related topics, so I decided to leave journalism and spent a year working for a nonprofit that coordinated services to address homelessness.

Over the years, I managed to stay in touch with Robert. He has lived in a boarding home for three years, his longest stay anywhere in decades. And he has stayed clean. Robert continues to speak up at city council, county commissioners and other civic meetings about the latest plans to address homelessness, and the need for housing and bus passes for people experiencing homelessness. These days he doesn't need to get arrested or fake chest pains to have a place to stay.

Roger Camp *is the author of three photography books including the award-winning* <u>Butterflies in Flight</u>*, Thames & Hudson, 2002 and* <u>Heat, Charta, Milano</u>*, 2008. His documentary photography has been awarded the prestigious Leica Medal of Photography. His photographs are represented by the Robin Rice Gallery, NYC.*

Old Swiss Watch Factory

Prior to the pandemic, I spent a month in Yerevan, the capital city of Armenia, as a guest of a former student. His apartment overlooked an abandoned watch factory, one of hundreds of derelict factories scattered over Armenia left behind when the Russians departed. Every morning I would watch the sun rise and light up the skeletal remains of the factory's sign which drew my attention to it as a photographic subject.

One advantage of living across the street from the factory was all the taxi drivers in Yerevan knew where the "old Swiss watch factory" was. Given my limited Armenian, it was all I had to say when I wanted to return to the apartment.

There is a very interesting anecdote about the factory I was told by the locals. When the factory was operational it assembled watches which were then shipped back to Russia and disassembled. The parts would then be shipped back to Armenia and the cycle would begin again. This was done to keep workers employed in both Armenia and Russia.

This is not as far-fetched as it might sound, but you have to decide for yourself if it is true!

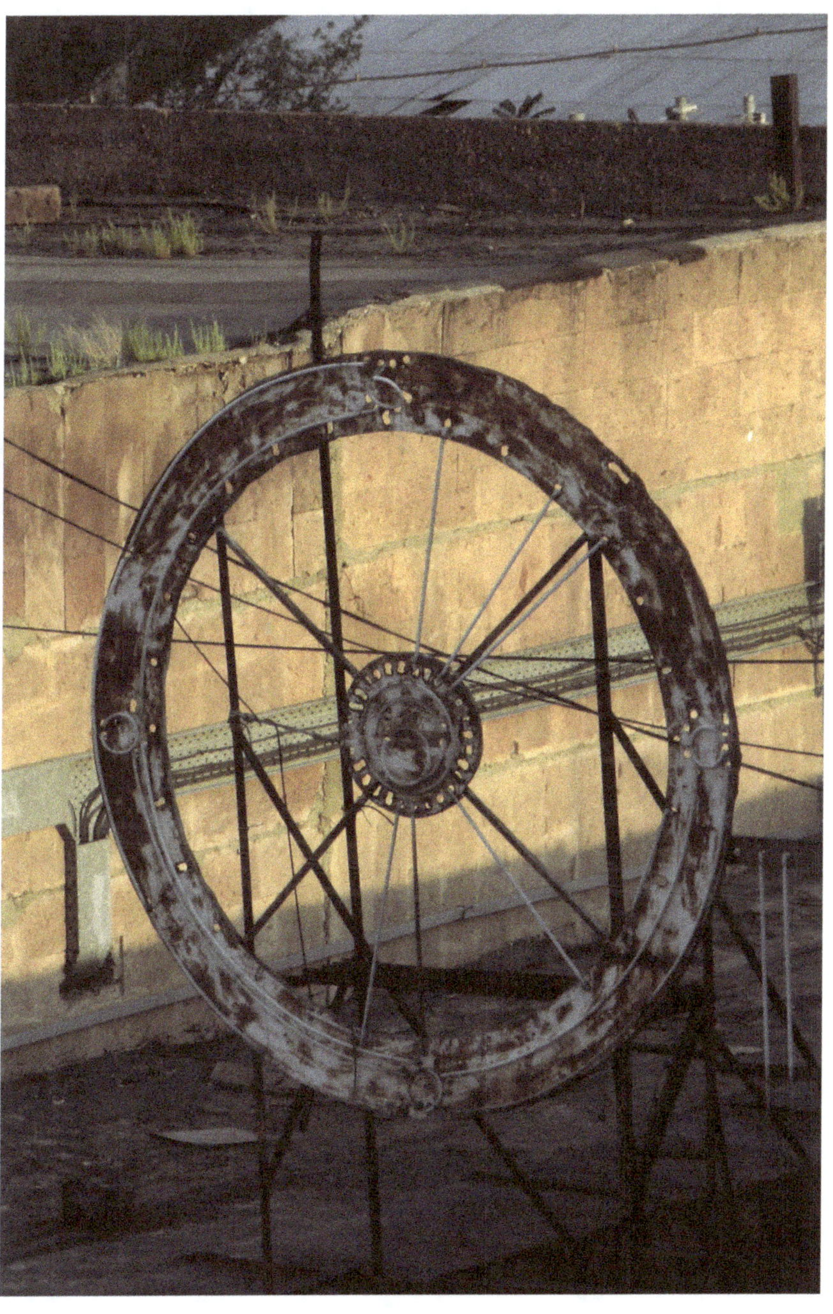